# Praise for Patrick Holland

## *The Mary Smokes Boys*

Longlisted for the 2011 Miles Franklin Literary Award
Shortlisted for *The Age* Book of the Year
A 2011 *Australian Book Review* Book of the Year
A 2011 *Adelaide Advertiser* Book of the Year
A 2011 *Readings* Book of the Year

*The Mary Smokes Boys* is a gem. The writing is absolutely terrific and the characters distinct and deftly revealed. This story is a heart wrecker.

BARRY LOPEZ, author of *Light Action in the Caribbean*

Patrick Holland's beautiful, beautiful novel is a tale that transports you through its realisation of place and its genuinely affecting story of love (for brothers, sisters, mothers, fathers). And yes, for a language as pure and magical as I have read in a long time ... A major work.

MARTIN SHAW, *Readings* newsletter

One of those books, one of those straight-to-the-heart, life-changing books.

KRISSY KNEEN, author of *Affection*

Barely a scene or image is wasted ... He weaves Hemingway's blunt sentences and carved dialogue with the old fashioned storytelling of a folk tale imbued with the dark romance of a Nick Cave ballad.

JO CASE, *The Age*

# The Darkest Little Room

*Pulp Curry*'s Top 5 Crime Books of 2012

This both a stunning page-turner and an investigation into the dim caverns of the human heart and soul that bears comparison to Graham Greene and Joseph Conrad. Holland is, quite simply, one of the best prose stylists working in Australia today.

MATTHEW CONDON, author of *The Trout Opera*

Patrick Holland has joined the ranks of the adventurer novelists and enhanced his growing reputation.

MICHAEL ROBOTHAM, author of *Say You're Sorry*

In many ways, *The Darkest Little Room* is the perfect 21st-century Australian novel, exposing the cruel underbelly of life in the Asia-Pacific region while also managing to be a cracking read.

CHRIS FLYNN, *The Age* and *Sydney Morning Herald*

Patrick Holland will be one of Australia's greatest writers of the future. I can't say you heard it here first because everyone is saying it.

KRISSY KNEEN, *The Sunday Mail*

This is a wonderful book, destined for the shortlists.

LISA HILL, *ANZ Lit Lovers*

Wonderfully drawn characters, acute and often painful observations about the expatriate condition, a vivid depiction of Vietnam, and a break-neck plot make this a mesmerizing read.

ANDREW NETTE, *Pulp Curry*

*The Darkest Little Room* ... is as gripping and thrilling as it is effortlessly artistic and lyrical. Many titles these days are billed as literary thrillers but this one truly fits that description. *Book Rating*: The Story 4/5; The Writing 5/5.

BOOKLOVER BOOK REVIEWS

There is a directness and spareness to the prose that beautifully balances out the action and the more traditional elements of the plot, and the slow, meditative tension easily calls to mind the dark romance of Greene's *The Quiet American*.

JESSICA AU, *Readings*

## *Riding the Trains in Japan: Travels in the Sacred and Supermodern East*

Shortlisted for the 2012 Queensland Literary Awards, Best Nonfiction
Shortlisted for the 2012 Courier Mail People's Choice Award

*Riding the Trains in Japan* succeeds in the difficult task of offering the reader a fresh vision of places and histories, of catching the impression of distant voices and also of offering the kind of insight only acquired through travelling.

THE AUSTRALIAN

## *The Source of the Sound*

Winner of the 2010 Walter Scott Price
Shortlisted for the 2011 Steele Rudd Prize

Beautiful and bittersweet ... written in tough lean prose, its denouement leaves a lingering impression.

SYDNEY MORNING HERALD

## *The Long Road of the Junkmailer*

Shortlisted for the 2006 Commonwealth Writers' Prize Best First Book
Winner of the 2005 Queensland Premier's Award, Best Emerging Author

A quite brilliant debut.

THE AUSTRALIAN

His imagination is unrivaled.

GOOD READING MAGAZINE

Quirky, magical, melancholic and utterly readable.

BOOKSELLER +PUBLISHER

Library of Congress
Cataloging-in-Publication Data

Hawthorne Books
& Literary Arts

Holland, Patrick, 1976–
The Mary smokes boys / by Patrick Holland.
pages cm
ISBN 978-0-9893604-0-1
1. Australian fiction.
2. Families–Fiction.
3. Grief–Fiction.
4. Brothers and sisters–Fiction.
5. Domestic fiction.
I. Title.
PR9619.4.H65M37 2013
823'.92–dc23

9
8
7
6
5
4
3
2
1

2201 Northeast 23rd Avenue
3rd Floor
Portland, Oregon 97212
hawthornebooks.com

*Form*:
Sibley House, Bklyn, NY
Printed in China
Set in Paperback
First American Edition

*This book is for Racheal*

ALSO BY PATRICK HOLLAND

*The Darkest Little Room*
*Riding the Trains in Japan*
*The Source of the Sound*
*The Long Road of the Junkmailer*

# The
# Mary Smokes
# Boys

A Novel

**Patrick Holland**

HAWTHORNE BOOKS & LITERARY ARTS
*Portland, Oregon* | MMXIV

Tarry ye here, and watch with me.

MATTHEW 26:38

# One

# I

GREY NORTH LOOKED DOWN TO THE LIGHTS OF THE CITY'S winter exhibition. Mechanical rides flung children and lovers across the dark, and their delighted squeals could be heard even from the hospital. A pair of nurses crossed the corridor between rooms. One whispered "poor boy" and vanished. Grey's newborn sister took her troubled sleep in a room at the end of the hall. His sister was always to be called Pia, but now would be called Irene after her mother.

A rocket was launched at the exhibition grounds. The rocket slithered high into the sky and burst in a brilliant gold spider's web. Grey followed the falling embers to where a procession of cars' red tail-lights meant the end of the night.

His father came into the corridor and smoothed his thinning hair with his hand.

"Come see your sister, boy."

But Grey did not shift from the window.

"It wasn't because of her. Your mother wouldn't stop bleeding."

She had been only twenty-six years old. He had come home from school and she lay bleeding on the floorboards.

"Her heart gave out, boy. It was just – terrible luck.'

Grey was ten years old and did not believe his mother's heart would give out on its own. Something could have saved her.

"William North," a nurse called down the corridor. The

man acknowledged her with a nod and the nurse took his arm and led him to a room where he would speak with the doctor.

Grey watched the last of the fireworks bloom in the window pane.

THE INFANT IRENE was kept overnight for observation and Grey and his father stayed at one of a row of northern suburbs airport motels. It was a franchise motel with clean standardized rooms for people who had been somewhere and would soon be going somewhere else. A place between the places life was. At the motel you could be exempt from life. It was impersonal and soporific. They spent two nights at the motel and Grey did not cry. Out the motel room's one window were waterlogged flats, the flare of a distant oil refinery, a long and lighted bridge proceeding into the dark.

THE NURSES AT the hospital tried to impress upon Bill North some rudiments of infant care. They suggested a home-calling nursing organization and a pediatrician whose names he would not remember. They gave him pamphlets and wrote names and telephone numbers in his notebook.

Grey and his father spent another night at the motel where Grey did not cry.

WITH HALF THE money he had in the world Bill North arranged for his wife's body to be returned to their home.

On the evening of the drive home Grey did not speak. The infant Irene sat between her brother and father in a bassinette in their truck.

Grey watched the brilliant city dissolve into the industrial western outskirts. Neglected parks. Commuter tract wastelands. Concrete brothels bearing names of flowers in neon – Tiger Lily, Lotus, Sakura. Colossal empty shopping centers whose monoto-nous geometry invited vandalism. Wisps of juvenile gangs at the edges of shadows and inside dim culverts. A degraded passage through which Grey admitted the consoling dream of the world broken.

After the outskirts, Highway 54 ran through rolling country, ever emptier, until the dark was broken only by spare dots of light adrift on the horizon. Then came the family's home in the Brisbane Valley. Mary Smokes was a town surrounded by blowing fields. In the west was a broad corridor of flatland before the Great Dividing Range before immense inland plains. North and east were lakes and a filigree of rivers and the D'Aguilar Range.

Wide and empty country in which the world had no interest.

Bill North turned his truck north off Highway 54 and drove across a rail line onto the Brisbane Valley Highway. A half-dozen men were loading horses in a yard close to the road. Grey's father stared out his open window but did not slow the truck. The truck's headlights brushed the man Grey had heard his father call Tanner. Grey looked back at the obscure shapes of men working in only the deck-light of a bodytruck. He wondered if the horses were stolen.

Further north along that road, a mile south of town proper, was their house, a weatherboard cottage beached by an ocean of plain. Grey got out of the car into the cold and looked up at the stars. Silence and darkness made the stars fierce. A sleepless horse walked the fenceline, rattling the wire as it brushed and leant across it to the green pick in the Eccleston houseyard next door.

BILL NORTH LIT a wind-guttered candle on the kitchen windowsill. Without its orb of light, without the window, were the hills that channelled wind like water and the emptier plain and the silence that the wind tore into, and there all human attempts to reassure the eye and know the dark were swallowed. He lit the potbelly stove with rolls of newspaper and mixed powdered milk in a saucepan on the stovetop. He took a block of boxwood from the pile beside the stove and pushed the block into the coals.

There were three people beneath the roof before and

three people now, but the house seemed utterly empty to Grey. One wall was darkened by the smoke of a lamp that the first Irene North burned beneath a print of the Black Madonna of Częstochowa. Grey saw the stained wall and he burst into tears.

His father filled a glass baby's bottle from the stove, but Irene did not suckle as the milk was too warm.

GREY WENT TO sleep in his room lit blue by the moonlight that flowed through the window beside his bed. Before he lay down he looked out the window at the boys both he and his mother called the wild boys. They were walking across the haying grass to Mary Smokes Creek from Eccleston's. When the wild boys disappeared he slept. But late in the night he woke with terrible dreams and realised that his mother was dead, and he went to his father's room.

Bill North was exhausted and did not wake when Grey climbed in and lay down beside his sister. He put his finger in her tiny hand that gripped it. For the first time in his life his hand seemed large, someway closer to the hand of a man. He whispered in her ear that he hated her. Then he cried. Then he kissed her cheek. He fell asleep with her hand in his, tears running down his face onto the pillow.

# II

GREY'S SCOTTISH PRESBYTERIAN GRANDMOTHER DRESSED him in corduroy pants and a black felt jacket. His grandmother stared at him with unyielding cold blue eyes.

"And this is the best coat you own?"

"Yes, Grandma."

Bill North pretended he did not hear. He busied himself whittling a pencil with no intention to write.

"You poor boy. You must remember your mother did her best with what little she had.' Then to the man, 'You never can trust a priest, can you? When will Cooney be here? It's Saturday, so I suppose he's hung-over."

"I've got no more love for papists than any of the rest of 'em," said Bill North. He squeezed his temples and ran his hand over his weathered face that had lately begun to smooth with the retained fluid of a drunk. "I'm only doing as she would have wanted."

The old woman affected a sigh and telephoned the district Women's Committee about catering for the wake.

Grey looked into his father's eyes that were dull and defeated.

GREY STOOD IN the drafty timber church, uncomfortable in his clothes. Tears made his face red and hot despite the cold that whistled in through gaps in the wallboards. Through the service he wept until he could not breathe. He heard snatches of Father

Cooney's arid and assuasive sermon on the resurrection of the dead, and he did not feel God was in the room. Outside the church, people made apologies for death. If there is a God, Grey thought, then He is something wilder and fiercer than this.

THE CEMETERY WAS at the southeast edge of town below Solitary Hill. The wind blew rusty eucalypt leaves to bank against the fallen wrought iron fence. Beyond the cemetery was rolling yellow grassland where felled and windthrown timber was scattered amidst spare, ringbarked trees. Buffel and feathertop grass grew out of cracks in the gravestones. In the northeastern distance the hills darkened under a sweeping cloud, and mist pooled high in the mountains.

Grey stood before everyone, isolated as an object of pity, in a rare, cold spitting of winter rain. His jacket looked even shabbier after it was wet. Black dye ran from the sleeves into his palms. His over-long hair was pasted to his forehead. He wished very much to be away from the crowd. Men he vaguely knew came to shake his hand. Chalk-faced women he did not know at all kissed his cheeks. The women stroked his wet head and looked very sorry. His grandmother wore a wrathful expression with no certain object. At finding themselves accidentally near her the other mourners shuffled away to a safer distance. Bill North looked stunned and held his head and his hands.

A FEW OF the chalk-faced women began singing "Abide with Me," but like a too-delicate candle, the song faltered and was extinguished by the wind. The singers left along with everyone else for the wake at the town hall.

Grey crept away. He did not want the others at his mother's grave and was glad when he saw they were leaving without him. He sat alone in the grass outside the yard. He was nauseated by the thought of the wake, that empty formality he had witnessed when his grandfather died.

At her father's funeral Grey's mother had told him of the

vigil over the dead in the early Irish Church, on terrible islands of rock where anchorites went to be alone in the presence of God. Now, despite his few years and no history or remembrance of anything but a story told him by his mother, he dreamed of that ritual, though he could give it no certain shape, merely commingle symbols of solemnity: candles; heaving dark song; hooded faces; a howling wind that somehow did not put out the candles. But this afternoon there would be a polite and nervous hour of tea and cake before the townspeople hurried to their houses, where death would leave them be. This rather than an all-night watch with eyes in the shadows: men watching for ... He did not know.

I will stay awake, Grey said to himself.

He watched his grandmother and three women in conference. They looked about the cemetery for him. They looked across the plain. A Mary Smokes school teacher cast her eyes in his direction. The woman would think he had run off for attention. She would offer him some tranquil consolation. He did not want to be consoled. He stood up against the grey sky and thought of running to the west, where the emptiness seemed interminable and offered infinite escape. But the concerned, pitying look on the woman's red face arrested him.

# III

IN THE NIGHT HE LEANT AGAINST THE HILLS HOIST IN
the houseyard. He watched wet oats and feathertop glinting in
the broken light. He looked across Eccleston's to the paint-stripped
white house on stilts. The valley wind tore at the rusted corrugated-iron roof. A dappled mare stood at the gate. The wild boys
were there now.

The undulating Eccleston grassland was intermittent light
and dark and the wild boys trod across it.

Grey went to the edge of his yard and put his hands on the
barbed wire that trellised wild jasmine. The Eccleston boy
carried a kerosene lamp and the others followed, hooded in their
duffel coats.

He wondered should he go to them.

He let them disappear over a shoulder of the earth into the
places they knew.

If he went to them his grandmother might wake. She slept
lighter than his sister. She might wake if Irene cried, or wake
with her bronchial cough and walk past his room to the bathroom
and see him gone. She might have done so already. If he was to
be scolded anyway then he should have gone.

The wind rent a gap in the cloud and let moonlight fall on
the path of the boys on the last crest before Mary Smokes Creek.
The clouds closed and the land was dark and the wild boys were
gone. I should have gone to them, he thought. A light came on
over his shoulder in the kitchen. He crept back inside unnoticed.

# IV

GREY WOKE EARLY THE NEXT DAY AND HIS GRANDMOTHER was sitting in a wicker chair by the stove. She slept no more than four hours in any night. Only her eyes shifted when she addressed her son-in-law. She told him to go into town to buy food, so she might go about the task of feeding his children.

Bill North said she could come and cook if she was determined to, but she was not to stay in the house. The old woman took no notice. And Grey watched his father turn his eyes to the floor. It was the same betrayal of guilt he had read in his father's eyes at the funeral and days before at the hospital. The atmosphere in the house was taut with a final accusation that was never made ...

GREY'S MOTHER AND father had lived apart beneath a common roof. Michael Finnain had insisted on the marriage after his daughter fell pregnant, despite the mother's protests. "Even our girl must own her actions," he said pitifully. "The child will be born and the two married, though it breaks my heart to lose her.' In marriage, Irene had found faith consoling; she recalled her soft-spoken father's admissions of the inevitability of sin and the need to accept original guilt. It made her load easier to bear, to think she was not paying for some extraordinary mistake that was hers alone. She prayed for forgiveness and forbearance before her icon cards of St. Magdalene and St. Pelagia ...

At fifteen she had kissed a boy she came to detest. She

wanted to eradicate the stain. Bill North saw her standing on the road in front of school in the rain with her books over her head. He drove her home in his truck. She felt important and romantic, and the next Friday afternoon Grey was conceived in the cabin of Bill North's truck at the edge of Lake Wivenhoe. Clouds floated along the water that evening while the young man lay beside her asleep with a half bottle of whisky still in his hand. A small timber row boat was pulled off its anchor and drifting near Cormorant Bay. Irene Finnain leant on the windowsill and watched the boat and cried.

Her father had taught her to speak Irish. She would have amazed her old aunts in that distant country she would never see. She played Bach's preludes and fugues and sang the canticles of Hildegard von Bingen. An Ursuline nun who trained in music at the Brisbane Conservatorium had taught her. Sister Marie Hauswald said no one in Mary Smokes knew how well the girl's voice carried the great prayers. When she married she rode with her piano and books in the back of Bill North's truck to her new house beyond the southern edge of town and every young hope she had in the world beyond vanished into the country's great emptiness.

She did her best to be a dutiful wife. To counter his feelings of inferiority, Bill North told her that their marriage and the child had kept him from a life he intended, though he could give no shape to that envisioned life; only that in it he was free from all duty. He spent his spare hours with boys from the railway. Most nights he saw no reason to come home early, or at all.

Grey had often sat up with his mother who waited by a cold plate of dinner. She would send him to bed before midnight. Then he would sit in the doorway of his room, listening to her praying until her husband returned.

Grey would not sleep if he heard her crying. He would remain in the corridor and if she saw him he would go to her and she would not send him to bed again. One night she wiped her eyes and turned down her icon lamp and took his hand and told

him about heaven. She made it sound like a palace in the sky with
a glass floor, so you could look down and watch over the ones
you loved. "Will Bill go to heaven?" – "Yes," she said. She said
everyone would be changed in heaven, so they were fit for it.
They would even change in appearance. He said he did not want
her to change; he asked how he would recognize her if she
changed so much. And the pretty girl of twenty-two smiled, "You'll
know me. You'll know me by the things I say."

"Were you praying for me again?' Bill asked when he
returned that hour and found her sitting in a chair beside the
Black Madonna.

His wife turned away from him.

"Ah, you were. That's why I'm home. Your God came and
pulled me by the ear. You must be a favourite of His.' He lit a cigarette and sat down in the dark. "I was just about to take from
Molly Small the thing that you can't give me. A slut she may be,
but she sympathises. She's a warm woman, where others are
cold as fish.' He began undressing and throwing his clothes over
a chair. "He's spiteful your God that doesn't exist. You must be
the most chaste girl that was ever knocked up at fifteen. Molly
thinks so. Well, now He's got you all to himself.'

Grey lay awake and listening.

Bill North left his food untouched in order to mock his
wife's sense of duty. He resented her for making herself a martyr
on his account.

He believed a racehorse might make him the wealth that
some-mysterious-how would free him. He went to sales and
bought the cheapest yearlings in the hope that one would be
lucky – he could give countless stories of unpredicted success
that had arrived on other men. He spent the family's money
on horse feed, veterinary bills and carriage to district races. And
what was left he drank. He squandered his wife's dowry and
borrowed another two-and-a-half thousand dollars from his
father-in-law that was never repaid. He bought a colt with good
bloodlines with Stan Eccleston, who was living with a black

woman next door. But Eccleston sold his share to August Tanner and left town for reasons no one knew and took work dropping bores in the far northwest of the state. Tanner was a horse dealer – in the phonebook he listed himself under "bloodstock agent" – but rumour said he sold whisky, black girls and guns as often as horses. Tanner and Bill North made poor partners and the horse was soon sold.

Bill North bought more than a dozen horses through Tanner, but none worked out, and finally he was convinced that Tanner had been cheating him for years, passing off horses he knew were faulty. One of the most promising had fallen dead in the paddock. Tanner blamed a snakebite that could not be found.

The only visitors to the house were Bill North's railways friends and a few local hands and horse workers who came for cards and drink. When they came Irene would sit on the back steps with Grey and name the constellations, though the boy's amblyopia meant he could not bring them into focus; else she would sing "Fhir a' Bhàta" or "O virga ac diadema," and she would not go back inside until the house was empty.

Bill North's friends teased him jealously about his pretty wife. One night a half-caste ringer made a joke regarding her and a hand of cards and Bill North broke the man's jaw and dragged him onto the road.

IRENE NORTH TRIED to teach her son the piano but he had no aptitude. He was sorry that this saddened her. "Perhaps when you're older," she hoped. And Grey nodded. He promised when he was older he would learn to play the piano, and even to speak Irish as she did. Occasionally she taught him a word or phrase, and her husband mocked her for teaching his son a language that was dying in its own tiny country half a world away.

Irene's consolations were her son and prayer, and walks on car tracks over the plain and on foot tracks she made herself through woodland. She collected wild flowering herbs in the rock outcrops that grew in the shade of the big grey gums. She sat on one that was fallen and watched the wind turning over the dry understorey leaves one by one, as though they were politely stepping into Mary Smokes Creek …

# V

IN THE EVENING BILL NORTH LEFT FOR WORK AT HELIDON
freight depot. Grey's grandmother resumed her station in the
wicker chair by the stove fire.

"What on earth are you pacing about the place for, boy?"

Grey shook his head.

"Something's troubling you?"

His sister cried. His grandmother rose and went to her
and rocked her to sleep. Grey waited. He poked the coals in the
stove with a long splinter of cypress pine. The old woman sat
heavily back down in the chair and wrapped a grey shawl around
her shoulders.

"Why did my mother die?"

"Many women died in childbirth in my day."

But a calendar on the wall said the year was 1985 and
Grey knew that number was a talisman against such disasters as
death in childbirth.

"Bill said it was her heart."

"Toxemia we called it when I was nursing in the war."

And Grey thought that this word sounded more like a cause
of death.

"Irene had it when you were born too. She survived it then.
It was not so severe. But we all knew she must never fall
pregnant again."

"Then why–?"

The old woman had gathered momentum now and her scruples fell away.

"Because your father could not keep his hands off her. Because his love was insufficient. Like a dog that plays with a kitten until it's dead, he had to maul her though it meant it would kill her. And then he left her ... he left her all alone. He should have had her in the city already. He should have been home. He should have left you home with her too."

The boy's eyes fell to the floor. He remembered the blood on the floorboards; how he could very nearly carry her; the hour he had taken to walk home from school that day ...

"But you were not to know."

IN THE NIGHT he knelt on his bed and faced the open window. He looked up at the stars and prayed to God that his mother would be returned to him, and this time he would be her keeper. I will stand between her and the world, if only You will trust her to me.

Grey prayed with tears in his eyes and finally the stars seemed to throb and the throbbing was in his heart and then, worn out with grief and the impossible distances out the window, he fell on his bed and slept.

# VI

WITH HIS MOTHER GONE GREY KNEW HE DID NOT BELONG to any family. So his thoughts turned to the wild boys of town, who could be found at any hour of night, for they had no careful guardians.

He had watched them every night since his mother's death, walking through land that was not theirs by any title, yet they claimed it as the last ones awake when the dark enfeebled all man's claims.

Grey imagined the nights of the wild boys charged with secret meaning. Such was their deliberateness in walking to the water, away from the world. So when all the lights in the house were out and his sister had stopped crying, Grey stepped quietly out of his room and buttoned his duffel coat and left by the back door.

THE SKY WAS high and cloudless and winter bright. The galaxy flowed from the southeast like a lambent river. He came to his back fence. The bent iron gate was rusted tight to its hinges. He put the toes of his canvas boots in the mesh and leapt into Eccleston's. He walked away from the road, northwest across shot-blade wheat and yellow grass toward the house where smoke was unravelling from the chimney. Eccleston's hairy, long-unridden Appaloosa followed him along the fenceline. White moths rose from the grass at every footfall.

He crawled through a barbwire fence and climbed the high

flight of stairs at the back of the house. He saw the Eccleston boy raise the glass of a kerosene lamp, turn up the wick and light it. Eccleston's step bore heavy on the floorboards, but there were no others in the house to wake at the creaking of the boards. The boy sat the lamp on the kitchen table and took a short-brimmed angler's hat from a nail in the wall and pulled his duffel coat over his shoulders against the wind that rushed through the open doors. Grey knocked on a wallboard.

"North!"

The boys knew each other, as all boys did in the town, though they had never been friends. Gordon Eccleston was five years older than Grey. And Grey had always been shy, a loner, a mother's boy ...

Eccleston was rarely at school. He collected wild limes and sold them to the Windmill Fruit Market till he could pay for a sheath knife and a set of rabbit traps. Once he had trapped a dingo in the mountains and brought it down to fight boys' dogs for bets. He scoured the country for sound windthrow and chipped off burls to sell to district wood turners. These were the visible ways he remained alive.

Eccleston's father was a good horseman. He had taught his son how to ride and how to work cattle. But the lessons were cut short when the man left town. The boy's mother, so it was said, was living in the ashes with some remnants of her people near the reserve at Cherbourg. It may have been calumny that said the boy's father had staked his own life on the turn of a card, and that this was why he was gone northwest, also that the boy was not truly the man's son, also that his Aboriginal mother's people had tried to kill him at birth for the trouble he might bring them.

Grey's mother had known the boy better than he. She spoke to young Eccleston on her walks – he was often on the river and in the woods. The first time she saw him she was walking along the burn-off at Mary Smokes Creek flat that was also the stock route. She came to a smoking van and tethered horse and saw a small half-caste child, wild-eyed and face caked with mud. He half-hid behind the van and watched her come. She asked him who he was and where he came from, but he remained silent and stared at her with the complicit curiosity and fear of a wild animal. She stayed with him until evening, when the sound of cattle treading on stick came through the scrub into the clearing.

The drovers who tailed the cattle found a spider-thin girl in a calico dress at their camp, barely showing the six months she had been with child, and holding the filthy hand of the half-caste boy who a week before had shown up at their fire just as unannounced as she did now. The drovers told her they did not know who the boy was or where he had come from or even his name. He had just taken to following them like a dog. Their woman meant to drive him in to the police that day, but he had run off and hidden in the woods, and she had gone to town without him. They told Irene North she was welcome to him, then watched her lead the boy across the burn-off in a spitting of rain that raised clouds from the ash on the ground.

She did not give the boy over to the police but to the only Aborigine she knew, Possum Gallanani, who lived on the other side of the creek, and was then building horse yards for Stan Eccleston. Possum took one look at the boy and sighed and claimed to know him and claimed the boy belonged to his "cousin," Beatrice. He said he would ask his boss for a car to go get her. He said the boss would give it. The next morning the wiry-haired black woman appeared on the Norths' doorstep. And that night woman and child were living next door.

Grey's mother did not tell the authorities when finally the boy was left alone. She had witnessed the bleak humanity that the government delivered to the half-caste children of the district. After Stan Eccleston left, she and one itinerant nun made sure the boy was alive. Irene would have taken him in at dinner, only she was afraid of his possible influence on Grey. She was ashamed of her fear, especially when her husband caught her taking a slice of corned brisket to the Eccleston house and warned her it was not his duty to feed the delinquent black boys of the country. Once Grey had seen his mother stroke the Eccleston boy's head …

Now he stood in the house he was never allowed to visit. A blue bitch walked across the kitchen to retrieve a rotten shin bone from a cardboard box. The wind fluted through the chimney flue. Sawdust and ash were scattered at the base of the potbelly stove. Leaning against the stove was a chair with two sawn-off legs.

Eccleston saw Grey staring at the chair and smiled.

"Last night got cold."

THEY SAT AT the top of the back stairs.

"Smoke?"

Grey nodded and Eccleston lit two cigarettes at his lamp. The younger boy drew hard and choked and Eccleston smiled.

He said they would go to light a fire on the creek tonight. Despite the season the creek was running with rain fallen in the west. In only a day it would be winter-still again.

They sat in silence until seventeen-year-old Nyall Thiebaud arrived in a station wagon with his younger brother Matt.

Nyall came holding a bandaged hand before his face.

"Caught a splinter the size of a butter knife," he said.

"They milled late tonight," said Eccleston.

Nyall shook his head.

"I bin at the hospital. Severed an artry. Went to the bone."

Eccleston sucked his teeth.

In his good hand Nyall held a bottle.

"Finest Scotch whisky eight dollars can buy."

"Good painkiller," said Grey, quoting a man who came to his father's card game.

Eccleston and Nyall agreed. Grey smiled and looked at his boots and spat off the stairs.

"This is Grey North. From next door."

Eccleston pointed to the yellow cottage across the way.

"You're the one whose mother died," announced Matt Thiebaud.

Grey nodded.

Eccleston threw away his cigarette butt and furrowed his brow. Grey saw he had not known. Each fixed the other's eyes. Grey nodded.

"Ah, hell," Eccleston whispered. "Ah, hell," until his whispers were silent.

Off the road and down the gravel drive came treading a long-gaited boy who Grey knew was Paul Offenbach – the way the boy pronounced his name would have been unrecognizable to his grandfather. Behind Offenbach waddled part-simple Raughrie Norman.

Offenbach indicated his companion with a flick of his hand.

"Look what I found on the road!"

Raughrie Norman's strawberry-blond hair blew across his bespectacled face in the chill wind. His slightly prognathic jaw jutted with the excitement and frustration he felt among the boys, of wanting very much to speak and having nothing to say. Norman was shuffled between grades for English and Art at Mary Smokes School. His teachers were perpetually undecided on the question of where he was least awkward. Sometimes he attended the special school at Toowoomba, though mostly he wandered without purpose from class to class at the school in the town where he was born and would never leave.

ECCLESTON TURNED DOWN the lamp wick and left the lamp at the top of the stairs and pushed down his hat. The boys buttoned their duffel coats and pulled up their hoods and walked east to Mary Smokes Creek. Eccleston had dragged his left foot since the age of ten, when he was hung up in a stirrup pulling cleanskins out of the hills with his father, and he dragged it now across the country his father had years ago sold to August Tanner.

The wind beat a loose sheet of shed iron in the north and hushed in the grass. When the wind dropped there was the sound of the stars: the immense and ancient roar of silence.

They took the steep descent, holding onto grass and trees,

steeping sideways in unsure footholds, treading on stairs of
tallowwood roots and petrified wood, and along a narrow footpath
in the brush down onto the bend. At the bend a strip of gravely
beach stepped into a slow-running pool that was sheltered by a
jutting of earth and a lighting-struck red gum.

Slabs of granite and basalt were settled in the bed and the
water purled around them, though in time of heavy flood you
heard the rocks grinding, the water turning them over. The water
pooled and then riffled over rock and gravel bars both up and
downstream of the bend. Debris was piled eight feet high on the
branches of a she-oak on the outer curve.

"When'd the creek ever get that high?" – "When we were
sleepin." – "When were we asleep?" – "The water knows when
we're asleep. Then it rises." – "You think it knows?" – "The water
knows. I seen bridges either side of ere where the water bent
and snapped steel posts set three feet deep in em. And always at
night when no one's watchin." – "That's true, I've seen that." –
"The water knows all right."

A pencil of moonlight breached the trees and lit the creek.
Winter's scant water was the colour of coffee, but the rain that had
fallen upstream had turned it clear. In summer the boys would
sit in crystalline water, backs against the bough of the fallen tree,
or against the riffling rocks and boulders, else upstream a little
where the roots of a giant spotted gum cradled and held up a
section of the stream and made a waterfall and pool like a bath,
where you could nestle in and let the water spill over your head
and rest your elbows on the roots. But the boys would not swim
now in August.

They lit a fire of windthrow and sticks on the bank. They
found a log of eucalypt. The eucalypt log was long to catch but
when it caught they would have sweet-scented fire all night and
coals for tomorrow night too.

The creek murmured.

Grey thought about where the course of the water was

unknown to him. The splintering creeks and gullies west of here, in the mountains and across the plain.

Mary Smokes Creek had captured the headwaters of creeks in the north, leaving misfit streams in the valley and wind gaps in the hills, and this course that was barely known and kept water through most of the year. The creek met the Brisbane River south of Lake Wivenhoe. Then the water skirted the range and wound through the city before emptying into the Pacific. The big river's current was strong, but not as it had been before the Middle Creek section was dammed to keep the city from being washed into the sea. Grey's grandfather had told him that in 1893 men saw a fifty-foot wall of floodwater strike a cliff at Caboonbah and felt it shake the earth. A rider was sent to the nearest town to warn the city, and the wire he sent that Friday afternoon stayed pinned to a post office noticeboard, unheeded over a carefree Brisbane weekend, until the city flooded famously. The Valley's big artificial lakes with European names – Wivenhoe and Somerset and Manchester – contained that water now.

The water's violence had grown quiet, stored like the violence of a candle flame. The water's secret was kept out here, hinted at in the rushing at Mary Smokes, in barely remembered high-water marks in the valley, and in the fierce southwest wind that poured from out of the plains across all the waters of this country, even shifting their courses. That wind carried weather that could darken the sky in an instant.

And all this, that they barely comprehended themselves, was the boys' secret at this hour of night. No one else in the universe was watching these waters. The boys and God were alone. Grey imagined they were the water's keepers.

NYALL THIEBAUD TOLD how at the mill that day he had been sawing she-oak when a dull tooth put his blade off course and the log bucked and then split, and had his hand not got in the way the splinter would have caught his face. The younger Thiebaud sipped the dregs of a bottle of green ginger wine and borrowed flippant toughness from his brother, nodding and cursing at everything the others said. Raughrie Norman had to be held back from leaping into the too-cold water. A girl had made fun of his slow speech at school that day and he would catch pneumonia to make her sorry. And Eccleston–who the older boys called Ook– sat and smoked with a faraway expression upon his face, and Grey imagined he saw pain akin to his own there.

Eccleston spoke to him when they were out of earshot of the other boys.

"Your mother was the loveliest woman I ever knew."

Grey nodded.

"My mother's gone too. She was just an old black woman. Still … "

He told Grey how his mother and grandmother had baptized him here in this water and in the smoke of bulrushes. This water, the last course of Mary Smokes, was one of many sacred places his mother's people mapped.

"Where are the others?"

"I don't know," said Eccleston.

"Could Possum tell you?"

Eccleston was surprised the small boy beside him knew the old black man he called his uncle.

"Pos isn't from here. He doesn't even know what country he takes. My mother told me about gettin baptized here. In her own language too."

"You spoke it with her!"

He shook his head and took a pouch from his duffel coat and took a pinch of tobacco.

"There was a time I could understand it. That was years ago."

Eccleston said his grandmother spoke nine dialects. His mother, two.

"And you were baptized right here?' said Grey.

"I don't know." Eccleston licked the edge of a paper and sealed and lit a cigarette. "Somewhere round here."

Grey nodded and stared into the fire.

SO THE TOWN'S wild boys made some of their ocean of time significant. At Mary Smokes Creek; at Lake Wivenhoe; at the edge of the woods, building fires and scattering them with their boots. On the highway finally, walking on the edge of the asphalt in silence. They raised their eyes from their hoods to see the disconcerted look of late-night drivers who wondered what this sleepless tribe was and what it meant.

They walked to the top of Solitary Hill at the edge of town and caught glimpses of Highway 54, the faint glow of mercury-vapour lamps that reached beyond the purpose of the lights and into the dark of the boys.

# VII

GREY'S GRANDMOTHER WOKE IN THE MIDDLE OF ONE
September night and walked past his bedroom door and looked
in at an empty bed. When Grey returned from the creek the
yellow veranda-light was on and his grandmother sat in her wicker
chair watching him come. Thereafter she kept a careful watch,
rising at the slightest creak of the floorboards. She declared she
would not let her daughter's son become recalcitrant in her
absence. As a punishment she made him return directly from
school and did not allow him to see anyone except old Jack
Naprasnic the cabinet-maker, who Grey had taken up weekend
work for, stacking and polishing timber.

For amusement in the evenings Grey played with his sister.

Irene was hardly ever well. She suffered severe bouts of
croup that required treatment at the clinic in Toogoolawah and
nightly care at home with steam and camphor through the dry
winter. Her ailments and the absence of mother's milk meant she
took slowly to food and was underweight even into adolescence.

Grey pitied her. He ran his fingers through her dark hair
to make her sleep. He wondered that she looked so unlike his
mother.

To fill the hours before bed his grandmother told him old
stories. She spoke of her father. For Grey, that man's existence was
achieved chiefly by a painted photograph that had once greeted
him in the living room of his grandmother's house in town. The
photograph was of a fair-haired, femininely handsome man in

infantry uniform who shared certain features with Grey's mother. The man had fought in the Battle of Beersheba. The photograph was taken months before he was killed advancing on Damascus. Now it sat in a pile of such photographs against the skirting boards in the old woman's room. She often shuffled and meditated upon one or other of the pictures, though she did not ever hang them, as though it was pointless or blasphemous to decorate the awful present with the golden past.

Grey's grandmother spoke to him of a Celtic heritage, even of a pioneering Australian one, a Christian one – Protestant, never betraying the Catholic tradition of her husband, who she called "romantic and unstable like a woman." But Grey did not feel he possessed any heritage. His isolation – his embittered grandmother who was like a relic of something long passed, and his mute and broken father – meant that all he inherited was broken or delivered stillborn.

The one cherished thing bequeathed him by the past was the memory of his mother. He had never let his grandmother clean those wallboards darkened by the smoke of the icon lamp. Only to stories of his mother would Grey listen with rapt attention. So Margaret Finnain would set out through her private landscape of reverie, with Grey trailing in the shadows …

"Once," she chuckled, her eyes out the window, following the story she told to where it fled into the hills, "Irene looked all day for a mangy pet rabbit in the woods. Now *was* it the rabbit? – some such triviality. She got hopelessly lost and tore her ankles on an old flood fence, and when we found her in the evening, her face red and streaked with dirt and tears, she was sitting on a fallen crows ash beside a creek, cradling the thing in her arms, and laughing that she had prayed and the rabbit had come. Dreamy little girl she was. I asked her why she hadn't prayed for the way home … "

There was nothing in his grandmother's stories of how his mother had met his father, and Grey knew better than to ask. Nothing of how Bill North married her with a pinchbeck ring in the days when he was a part-time logger and railways boy and those boys had the run of the country. There was nothing of Irene Finnain's entrance into the world of adulthood – her few menial jobs, Grey's birth. Instead she remained ideal and untouched, at a vestal fifteen years old.

Grey knew his mother was the most beautiful girl who had ever lived. Her hair was blonde, with the enigmatic hues of the eucalypt woods in changing light, and her eyes were clear green like the lake after evening rain. She made old women sigh and children smile. At shire functions the children competed with each other to be closest to her, and vied for the right to hold her hand and skirt, and Grey's heart swelled when finally the prettiest creature anyone had ever seen let him lie across her lap while she listened to music or the conversation of others and ran her fingers through his hair.

But now, even so soon after her death, he could not always recall her face. He relied on photographs. He used his grandmother's stories to place her in familiar settings, as though her face might borrow solidity from the places. At night he would lie in bed and try to imagine her, and sometimes her face would not come. Then he prayed again, *bring her back to me*.

GREY WATCHED OUT his window for the boys. He saw Eccleston had walked off unaccompanied. Grey wondered if the other boys had deserted him. That could not be true. But so it seemed. He went to the back stairs. Eccleston carried no lamp. Grey could barely discern the boy's form in the scant light that escaped piles of October's clouds. Tonight Eccleston was not walking down to the bend in Mary Smokes Creek, but south toward the big highway.

Grey heard the chink of crockery and his grandmother's footsteps behind him.

For want of an explanation he pointed across the yellow grass. His grandmother's cataract-clouded eyes could not have seen the diminishing shape that was Eccleston, still she seemed

to know what Grey had pointed at. Strangely it seemed he was
not in trouble.

"You be careful making a friend of him. There's some in this
world that are destined for trouble. It's written in the book
before time. You see if I'm not right." The old woman sighed and
frowned.

She went to bed sure Grey was daunted by Calvin's hell.
But when he heard the rattling breath that meant she was asleep,
he pulled on his canvas boots and duffel coat and stepped
quietly down the stairs.

He stood at the barbwire fence. Though he was gone from
view now, Grey imagined Eccleston was bidding him to follow. If
he hurried he would catch him up.

THEY WALKED ACROSS a rolling wood of eucalypts and met
Mary Smokes Creek where it was a few fetid pools of amber
water. Much of the timber and rock had been removed from this
reach, so only floodwater stayed here for any time. They met a
dirt road that ran down from the hills to the Valley Highway.

"Where are we goin, Ook?"

"I've gotta get some money."

They walked to within hearing distance of Highway 54. They
pulled a gap in a barbwire fence and went through and walked
to the white house that belonged to August Tanner. Men and boys
sat on bonnets and stood beside a dozen vehicles in a ring on
graded dirt beside the house.

"Wait here," said Eccleston.

Grey stood at the edge of the dirt that was lit by a spotlight
mounted on Tanner's roof gutter. The light was trained on a point
in the centre of the cars. Eccleston walked through the light,
and Grey felt that Eccleston was sorry he had brought him. At a
glance Grey took in a gallery of grotesque faces. A man with a
stubble beard and a wide-eyed black man made some inaudible
joke and the white man's angular features gathered into a grinning mask.

GREY WALKED IN the dark around the backs of the vehicles and saw Eccleston standing at the door of a corrugated-iron shed, asking something of an old Aborigine who Grey knew was Possum Gallanani. When Eccleston went inside, Grey went to the window.

The shed was lit by one unshaded bulb that gave light enough to show a man taking cash out of a metal box. The lantern-jawed face and cropped grey head belonged to Tanner.

Grey heard muffled snatches of talk. Eccleston said he had no money left, he hadn't eaten. Tanner returned to the metal box and took out a note and handed it to the boy.

"Your old man can never say I didn't look after you."

But Eccleston said he needed more than that.

"Bloody hell, boy, you go through money." Tanner spat on the dirt floor. "We've got fights tonight, like you see."

"That's what I'm here for."

Tanner took back the note.

"I'll put this on you."

"Who'll I fight?"

"Rod Bates."

Rod Bates was distantly related to Tanner. The man called him his nephew. He had just quit school and was working at the abattoir north of Mary Smokes at Kilcoy. In the past he had run with the wild boys of Mary Smokes, though he had fallen out with Eccleston.

"Find someone else."

"You boys have fought before."

"Not for money."

"The only others here are two full-bloods come down from Cherbourg. One's a shithead kid who thinks he can't be beaten, who every bloke here'll see right off you'll wipe the floor with; the other's a ringer from Jondaryan who Pos calls his cousin – he'll wipe the floor with you."

"I won't fight Bates."

"You've only gotta scratch the skin to see all you halfies'a got piss for blood."

"Why him?"

"No one expects me to bet against him."

"They've seen me before."

"He can fight too."

Eccleston sighed and spat.

"Then put your money on him and I'll take a dive."

"And get my throat cut? You said yourself they've seen you before. I trust you to fight better than to dive."

"Who's makin your bet?"

"Pos. I've used Charlie Lemon too much. The bloke who runs the book is wakin up to it."

"You're a fool to use Pos. He'll tell someone without meanin to."

"They'd expect him to bet on you. It won't affect the odds."

"They won't expect him to have any money."

"Today's Friday. Even an Abo can hold onto a paycheck for a day."

GREY SQUATTED AT the front wheel of a truck and watched two fights between black boys. He watched Eccleston and another boy, who looked at least two years older, take off their coats and shirts and have their hands wrapped in cloth.

The boys raised dust so it was difficult to see. They fought three three-minute rounds. By the end of the second, Eccleston had been knocked down twice and was bleeding from more than one cut. Possum wiped the blood from Eccleston's face and Grey saw plainly the gash under his left eye.

At the beginning of the third round Eccleston took a blow to his left cheek that sent him stumbling onto a car bonnet and a man called out an insult from the ringside shadows and Grey ran onto the dirt, flailing at the boy who stood arrogantly over Eccleston who was on his knees now. Like all pensive, sentimental boys Grey moved swiftly to tears and violence. He stood shivering and crying in the ring. Even when Eccleston grabbed his coat sleeve and tried to pull him into the cars, he stood fast. He stood between Eccleston and his opponent while laughter came from all sides, and then three men were needed to pull him off the Bates boy who slapped him hard with the back of his hand. The men threw Grey back out between cars.

Grey watched bitterly at the edge of the fray, his face stinging, while Eccleston took a final beating.

Eccleston went to Tanner's truck and asked for the twenty dollars he was given at the start of the night and Tanner gave it.

"Though you didn't earn it."

Grey met Eccleston leaning against the shed.

Eccleston stammered, adrenalin still shaking his voice: "That bastard Bates's got too big for me."

He felt for the twenty-dollar note in his coat pocket. He showed Grey and shook his head. Cars were disbanding onto the dirt road and highway. Eccleston put on his coat. They saw Possum Gallanani leap up to the cabin of Tanner's bodytruck.

"You were right after all, boss."

To which Tanner said nothing. Eccleston stopped and stared back at the truck. Possum jumped down and got in a dented Kingswood with a half-dozen other Aborigines and Tanner drove his truck into the shed.

A gigantic Aboriginal woman was called to tend Eccleston's face. She flushed the wound clean then dabbed it with methylated spirits. She held a needle over a lighter flame and made three stitches with nylon fishing line and covered them with paper tape.

"Who'd Pos put his money on, Auntie?"

"Pos dosen av any money, boy!"

"Who'd Tanner put his money on?"

"How would I know?"

Once the cut was stitched Grey pulled Eccleston's coat sleeve.

"Let's go, Ook."

"Tanner knew I was gonna get beaten tonight."

Grey was settled now that the fights were over. The violence in his heart was burnt out, replaced by fatigue and the ache in his face where the Bates boy had backhanded him, and he wanted nothing but to leave.

"Maybe not."

"Did you hear who Pos bet on?"

"No."

"Tanner bet against me, North."

"Maybe not. What Pos said might have meant anything."

"He bet against me."

"What difference does it make now?"

THEY WALKED BACK to Eccleston's house and took a drum of tar and rolled the drum to the southernmost fence and poured the tar into the hayed-off grass along the fenceline and even into the rushes and scant trickle of Mary Smokes Creek. Eccleston knelt on the bank and struck a match and shielded it from the wind and lit the grass. It was all Tanner's country to the brink of Eccleston's houseyard, but the southwest wind that blew tonight would take the fire into Tanner's horse paddocks.

The boys watched the tar vapours flashing and the wind throw fire across the grass and throw sparks in the air and then the creek and fenceline were burning in a cross.

They heard Tanner's horses bolting and whinnying in the dark. A black horse cleared a fence in panic and bolted into the woods; another got caught in the wire that ripped its legs before the horse pulled the section down and followed its mate. The boys watched the creek, fire skipping along the banks. Then they watched the water on fire.

Grey stood beside Eccleston until sirens sounded on the road. The boys ran to the north, into the gallery woods of Mary Smokes Creek and out of sight.

# VIII

AFTER A FEW HOURS SLEEP THE SUN ROSE ON BLACKENED earth. Grey remembered the night as though it was a dream. But when he walked down to the creek and saw the banks were cinder and ash he knew it was true. Red eucalypt leaves fell into the ash that rose and drifted and fell as black snow. Iridescent coagula of unburnt tar floated on the water. Tanner's country was a black swathe.

In the glowing afternoon Eccleston came rapping at the door, yelling to come quick and that they were after him.

"Who's after you?"

"You've gotta help me, North."

Grey saw that the badly-stitched cut under Eccleston's left eye was weeping. Deep bruises had come into his face.

"If they get me this time they're gonna send me to Borallon." Borallon was the district remand home for boys. "I can't go back to the house. They're in there waitin for me."

Grey walked to the back veranda and put his head around a post and saw a police car parked in Eccleston's drive and a policeman leaning in Eccleston's doorway. The policeman went inside.

"How'd you get here?"

"When I saw em pull up, I ran. I lost em in the woods and followed the creek north. I went to Possum's but he wasn't there, and there was no food in his humpy. Then I walked back to here through the grass. And now they're sittin there waitin for me."

"I'll hide you."

"No good. They'll be round here searchin before the day's out. Get me some food so I can last a couple a days in the hills – till they get tired a waitin."

Grey went to the pantry and took a block of cheese, two cans of salmon and a half-loaf of linseed bread. He put these in his rucksack along with a canteen, a bedroll, a pair of metal mugs and a jar of leaf tea.

THEY HURRIED OUT Grey's front door and crossed the road and walked directly west to a stretch of obscuring timber that would take them into town. The walked through the timber then crossed the road again and walked onto the creek. They followed the creek north. They walked behind the town to the northern outskirts then met a road that went into the mountains. They hitched a ride with a young woman in a late-model car who had been visiting her parents' farm near Toogoolawah and was headed back to the city through the range.

They decided that the police might be patrolling the mountain road. They rode with the woman to the foothills and then went cross country on foot. They walked through fallen cattle yards and dry creeks and gullies and stands of red and white cedar that few men ever saw. They got as far as sweet-smelling Mount Glorious where ancient hoop and bunya pines stood together with black booyongs, tallowwoods and strangler figs, and the air was no more the dry brown air of the flat, but crisp mountain air.

A timber truck picked them up on a dirt road. The driver was mystified when the boys told him they did not want to go all the way to the city but instead wanted to be dropped just short of it at Jolly's Lookout over Samford Valley. They reckoned the entrance to the city was the first place the authorities would come looking for them once they realized they had left town. For all the boys knew, the great wind gap that cradled the sprawling northwestern suburbs of Brisbane was crawling

with policemen anticipating the arrival of two juvenile arson-
ists. Though looking down at the edge of the city, the vast spill-
way of light, they began to sense their insignificance, the city's
profound unconcern.

AT JOLLY'S LOOKOUT there was cleared ground and plenty of
dead wood to make a fire. They ate nearly all their food that night.
Eccleston walked into the forest and brought back a shirtful of
sandpaper figs.

"Careful of the sap," he said. "It's poison."

Grey cut thick slices of cheese with his knife and they
toasted the bread and cheese in the flames then wrapped the
salmon up inside. They made a billy of the empty salmon
tin and Grey filled it with water from his canteen and threw in
a handful of black tea and pushed it into the fire with a stick.
They drank tea sitting side by side on the bedroll and looked
down at the smoky valley, the gleaming of Samford's scattered
lights and, in the east, the tendrils of the big city.

Grey remembered the long, redundant outskirts he had
driven through after his mother's death. Motels, car yards,
prisons and highways made up the beautiful ribbons of light he
could see tonight. He wondered if their tranquil embrace would
ever touch Mary Smokes. He lay down to sleep and watched
them twinkling.

IN THE NIGHT a wild dog howled and the boys woke.

"You hear that?' said Grey.

"It's just a dog."

"I know. I was just wonderin if you were awake, that's all."

Their fire was gone to coals. Grey sat up and blew on the
embers and shifted a half-burnt log to the middle of the fire with
his boot. The log was charred enough not to give a flame visible
from the road. The dog howled again, long and mournful, and
Eccleston sat up too. A night wind channelled east along the

road and tore ash from the ends of the logs in the fire. The boys pulled their coats tight across their shoulders.

"I don't want to go to Borallon." Eccleston said. He lit a cigarette in the coals.

"We burnt some country," said Grey. "Set loose some horses. Eventually they'll forget about it. The police can't spend all their time answerin to Tanner."

He watched a truck approach and pass on the mountain road below their camp.

"Tanner deals in good horses," said Eccleston. "Who knows what the ones we spooked were worth. They were probably all through the hills by this mornin, cut to pieces, feet busted up on rocks."

"I doubt it," said Grey. "We'll be all right." Though he did not know.

"It's what I've done before though too." Eccleston sighed. "They'll add it up against me."

He told Grey about the night Possum was beaten half to death by a bikie gang in a watch-house while two policemen looked on. He said the police in this country were all crooked. "I hate coppers, Grey. You know, at Borallon even the teachers are coppers. Even the priest is a copper!"

"I hate em too," Grey said. More than once Bill North had come home from public bars with wounds he claimed were inflicted by police. Grey shifted closer to the heat in the coals. "But the priest can't be a cop."

Eccleston smiled sadly.

"I spose not."

"I wonder if they're chasin us – those blokes who were at your house?"

"Maybe. But it's late. And cept for that truck before, nothin's gone by on this road."

"They've probably left off for the night," Grey said. "Anyhow, we've got a start on em."

"Yeah. We've got a start on em."

Eccleston sighed and closed his eyes.

"You know, North, it seems like someone has always been huntin me. Always." Then he sniffled. Grey did not know if it was tears or the cold. Eccleston threw his cigarette into the coals.

Grey looked back toward the road that disappeared into the wood, looking for something that may or may not have been there.

"I'll stay with you, Ook."

Eccleston smiled and stared into the fire.

The only sound outside the fire was the hushing of the forest, the mountain wind rolling down into the valley.

Grey took a mouthful of water and passed the canteen.

"Where are we going tomorrow?"

"I don't know."

The wild dog had settled and the boys lay down again to sleep.

Grey lay facing east with his eyes open. The city seemed an impossible place. They had nowhere to go in the city.

IT WAS COLD and the sky had begun to pale in the east when two policemen came and chased the boys down where they ran into the woods. The policemen dragged them into a waiting car.

SUNLIGHT POURED DOWN HIGH CREEK BEDS AND THROUGH gaps in the trees. The forest twinkled with late afternoon light and chimed with birdsong. They climbed crude stairs of granite and fig tree roots up into the heathland and walked to the lookout atop Mount Tibberoowuccum. The boys sat for hours and watched clouds and the shadows of clouds float across the hills until the western plains where the clouds were blown away.

A smoky dusk gathered over them. Then the stars came. Lights were studded in the range and scattered sparely across the west. It did not matter that Mary Smokes was out of sight. Once he could see the D'Aguilar range Eccleston felt he was in his own country. He looked through a wind gap where his thoughts travelled to the town he grew up in.

A lonely firework was launched from the backyard of a house in the north, they wondered for what obscure celebration.

"How long you got left?' said Grey.

"Year'n a half. The end of school."

"What will they do about tonight?"

"Nothin I can't handle."

It was the third time Eccleston had gone walkabout to this nearest wild country to the boys' home. He did not mind the work they gave him at Borallon as a punishment. The boys stood in silence looking west, and there was something in their silence up here on the mountain that said they would play truant from the world all their lives. "My wild brother" they said to each other without a word.

# Two

# I

IN TIME NYALL THIEBAUD AND PAUL OFFENBACH LEFT
town. No new boys came to take their places. Grey North, Matt
Thiebaud, Raughrie Norman and the returned Gordon Eccleston,
who had left school for good and made his way shooting foxes
and ringing, were the last Mary Smokes boys.

When Irene was six years old, Bill North took work as a
boundary rider out west on the Jimbour Plain. The work offered
him solitude and escape. People said he was a strange man and
that you needed to be for that work; and that was the way of the
country: the young moved into the city, and the lost and old moved
further west or into rooms above public bars to be forgotten
among ghosts. If more than a fortnight separated jobs, Bill North
returned. But his spells at home were broken by long months,
and his children were as strangers to him.

All Irene's love was reserved for her brother. She would wait
in the house or on the stairs for him to return from work at
Jake Naprasnic's and nights with the boys. Sometimes she waited
until very late, long after Grandma Finnain had gone to bed.

Slow-burning grief and weariness worked on their grandmother. She grew frail and her indifference to the world became
complete. She was as anachronistic as the painted photographs
that sat in piles on the floor of her room. She was less strict with
Irene than she had been with Grey and did not ever force her to
bed, even when Irene began school. She knew her granddaughter
would not be settled until she heard Grey's boots on the stairs,

and the old woman often went to sleep leaving her sitting up by the window in the living room.

In summer Grey would come treading up the back stairs after swimming at the creek with the boys, and when Irene heard his steps she would go and stand in the corridor. Then he smiled at his un-pretty dark-haired sister, and she sighed and held his hands with the unreasonable relief that made him laugh – as though there were any danger out there in the country he knew so well. And if she had some secret to tell him she would wait until any hour, even until sleep overcame her and he found her with her head on her arms on the dining table. If she woke she would tell him whatever childish thing it was that had seemed so important, and he would laugh and send her to bed.

WHEN THEIR GRANDMOTHER died both children mourned her, though Grey took the loss harder. The old woman's dilapidated house in town was sold for pittance, and without her pension check they were very poor. Grey's part-time work at the cabinet-maker's and the occasional check mailed by their father kept them on the borderline of poverty. But shortly Grey lost his job. The work had dried up and Jake Naprasnic moved to Toowoomba to live in a nursing home near his only daughter.

When Irene was hungry and without money she would thieve a tin of beef stew or soup from one of the two general shops, and Grey would scold her until tears came to her eyes, but then scold her no more. She took to selling her mother's things to the antique shop for a fraction of their value until Grey caught her. Her clothes were scandalous, dirty and torn. She cut her own hair, like a boy's but for a long tress that fell over her forehead or over her ear onto her shoulder. She was pitied by Mary Smokes women. At times they resolved to report the family to whatever government authorities handled such cases, but Grey was growing into a man, some said, and then Bill North would return to the house sober after weeks away from hard liquor.

The first few days of any return from the west, Bill North

spent dry and racked with guilt; then he even attempted to love his children, who regarded him as an occasional boarder. But these spells, both of concern and sobriety, passed quickly, and the man decided it was better for all of them when he was away. After any longer than a fortnight at home Bill North would take to drinking himself into oblivion. One night Grey came home and saw his father lying against the living room wall and the floor-boards wet with urine.

Bill North's bitch had pupped twice in two years to wild dogs and the three pups of the last litter now nipped the heels of any visitor, even Sister Nivard, the Poor Clare who had started looking in on them. She came the night Grey found his father on the floor. In his sister's bedroom Grey saw Sister Nivard lifting Irene's nightdress and examining her painfully thin body for marks of abuse, and he knew he must do better.

In time Irene welcomed the aging Sister's visits. The girl habitually hid her father's whisky bottles in order to be safe from prying townswomen, but she did not hide them from the Sister, and the Sister was the only visitor the girl would not leave to the half-wild dogs.

Sister Nivard came to the house twice a week to bring bread and canned fish and soap, and perhaps bake the children a simple cake. She told Irene stories of missionary work in India and of the nature of angels according to St. Aquinas, to which the girl listened in rapture. Bill North asked the nun why God watched a girl who was devoted to him die in pain, and left him to live on meaninglessly. He did not expect an answer. Sister Nivard only sighed and her fading blue eyes, set in a face that had never known adornment, stared out the window across the grassland.

Their father believed in nothing, so Catholicism, with all its ritual, hagiography, Latin prayers and icons, had about it the whiff of rebellion. Despite the Sister's insistence on moderation, Irene would fast on bread and lemon juice every Friday and fast totally on Good Friday and Holy Saturday, taking nothing but a little water, so by Saturday's end she was apt to faint. She prayed the Sorrowful Mysteries of the Rosary before her mother's icons, lit by candles she bought with money stolen from her father's wallet, and her frail body would excite Grey's pity.

Irene's religion was a thousands-of-years-old Eastern book she could barely read; fierce-eyed, long-bearded or serenely feminine, miracle-working saints; but also the slow, silent words she claimed were spoken by the stars; the spirits in the trees; the little waterfall called Wooroolin, deep in the woods, which she declared was sacred. She said at Wooroolin the scent of the water moved against the wind, and there were hours when the falling water made no sound.

She claimed she could see paths lit for her in the deepest corners of the woods. It was true she seemed to have a map and compass always in her mind, even in country she had not seen. She never became lost or frightened, no matter how far she walked, no matter how late. She knew how to follow the creeks and she knew by the shape of the country where they would lie, like one who had spent years there. She knew the stairways of granite and exposed tree roots in the mountains; the lie of lost and forgotten cemeteries; the wild mulberry bushes and wild orange trees where she harvested fruit in its season.

She would play truant from school and sit all day watching the clouds, else sit on Mary Smokes Creek from morning until dusk, calling birds to her hand. Some evenings there would be a phone call to the house to say she had been seen on a stretch of a man's country, and Grey would drive to collect her. Then he would find her wending her inscrutable way through waves of hay and barley in the dusk, just like the lost simpleton people took her for. And in the night she and Grey would sit together on the splintering back stairs and watch the stars and listen to the wind jangling their half-fallen back fence and soughing in the eucalypts and she-oaks on Mary Smokes.

At school she stood in Grey's shadow amidst the other sixteen- and seventeen-year-old boys, only reluctantly parting

with him to join children her own age when the bell rang for
class. She waited faithfully each afternoon for him by the school
gate. She would miss the bus rather than leave without him –
causing them to have to walk home together.

A jesting rumour persisted that Irene was not Bill North's
daughter, but rather the daughter of the middle-aged Vietnamese
cook at Mary Smokes' Chinese restaurant. It was encouraged
by the colour of Irene's hair and the friendship she had struck up
with Minh Quy's daughter, Amy. The two loners had paired
up and, once Grey had left school, they often played on the lawn
beside the restaurant after class. Old Minh would give Irene
dinner and sometimes there was enough for Grey.

Irene's hair was black and her face ghostly pale. Her body
remained excruciatingly thin even into her mid-teens. Grey
guessed this last condition was due to the sicknesses she had
suffered. Yet the curious thing about her appearance was not that
she must ever bear the marks of infant frailty, but that at the
same age her mother's hair had been white-blonde and her skin
olive in the ideal Australian fashion. Grandma Finnain said
Irene showed Black Irish blood, a strain of old Celtic via Iberia,
but when the girl misbehaved she recalled her Scottish grandfather dealing with a family of reviled Polish Jews from Minden,
who for want of companions interbred with Chinamen. They
were called Noschkes, and the old woman guessed North was an
Anglicisation of that name … More than one lost language,
more than one people and history flashed briefly in Irene: in her
sharp Celtic tongue, and the deep and whispering Hebrew eyes
that always seemed to be looking far away, from the border of
this world into some other. In Grey, so far as he could see, these
were mute, vanished.

THEIR FATHER DID not return to stay permanently at Mary
Smokes for seven years, after his horse fell on his leg on the
Dumaresq River. He had been working for cash and could claim
no pension. He was forced to take up work at the Helidon railway

again, with half the duties he had before and only a dozen hours' work a week.

By this time Irene had made of Grey a father, brother and closest ally, and welcomed her father home as one would a distant and barely-recognisable uncle. Bill North did not recognize his daughter either – she had lost her infant manners, dictates of her once sickly body. Now, by turns, she was the most vivacious and most solemn of young girls.

Feeling he had lost something never properly valued in time of possession, Bill North tried on occasion to reclaim the small part of his daughter's affections that had been his, but the attempts were in vain.

For feminine companionship and domestic service he married a divorcée, the daughter of an old man he once worked for called Teal. The woman worked as a waitress at Minh Quy's restaurant. One night when collecting Irene, Grey brought his father along to put some food in his system to counter the drink. Bill North's wife-to-be was smoking a cigarette and leaning against the back wall of the restaurant, staring into the small-town night.

Bill North and Angela Teal married in a registry office on the outskirts of the city. On the third night of their North Coast honeymoon the woman was shocked to discover they had run out of money. She drove in tears to her sister's house in the city and did not return for days …

NOW GREY FELT pity for the poor lame man who sat in the living room in the dying afternoon light, staring out the window while the wife he did not love and who did not love him spent yet another weekend at her sister's, the man asking his daughter, who indifferently refused, to come sit by him and talk.

THE NIGHT SKY was high and cloudless. Grey walked across the windblown stretch of grass and spare deadwood that he had walked since boyhood. Eccleston's two barely-ridden horses, the

smoky-blue gelding and old Appaloosa mare, walked along
the roadside fenceline. Grey climbed the low hills and walked
into the trees and stepped down the tallowwood roots to the bend
in Mary Smokes Creek.

He sat down with the boys on the strip of sand and gravel.
It was warm and there was light enough without a fire tonight.
They sat in a vivid dark.

Matt Thiebaud told Eccleston about some country in the
north that he could get them onto to shoot, where a couple of
young blokes might make a living, at least for a while before coming home. He said he was sick of working at the abattoir at
Kilcoy and of fencing at Tiger Scrub with the boy called Jack Harry,
who he said was as thick as the posts he strained wires to. He
spoke through the rolled cigarette that he kept always intact in
his mouth and squinted his pretty blue eyes. Grey was not listening. He squatted on the bank and watched the water purl
around rocks and shake the stars. The water ran deep and fast
around the bend, and faster over the gravel bar where Raughrie
Norman stood.

Norman, who the boys called "Flagon," fell fully-clothed
from the bar into a deep pool. Eccleston hung his clothes in a
tree up the bank and stepped in at the bend and Thiebaud went
after him. Grey leant against the husk of a tree. He watched the
boys with their heads beneath the last granite step of a waterfall.
He hung his clothes on the husk and stepped in. The water had
come from somewhere other than their warm night, from the
high country of shattered rocks in the southwest, and he shivered
at its touch.

The night ran on and the water ran faster and spilled over
the rocks and timber and splashed the boys' faces. The creek had
broken its banks in a storm a week ago and scoured the country
and the water tonight spilled into the newly cut rills.

Eccleston, Norman and Thiebaud crawled and swam to a
downstream rock pool. A full moon scaled the eastern sky and
illuminated the boys. Grey was alone. He swam upstream

and sank into the pool beneath the cradling spotted gum root and rested his arms and let the water crash over him. He laughed to himself at this inconsequential, late-night-creek-swimming small-town life. At such times all thoughts of leaving or anything else belonging to that still-distant place called the future left him alone. The world still moved slowly at Mary Smokes Creek. At the creek you took in the infinite and nameless changes in the hours, and moving at the same speed as the earth there was not that whiplash of time and the death feeling that came with hours lost unwittingly in degrees of waking sleep. At Mary Smokes Creek there was time for everything, and no desire to do anything at all. For a year now Grey had taken what work there was in the country, a little horse work and shifts at Bizzell's service station at the edge of town. And that was all he and his sister needed.

Thiebaud burst from the water. Grey had been quiet for too long and the boys covered him with arm-fulls of creek. He slid into the deepest hole. He knew that he and these boys owned the night as ever. They were the *dramatis personæ* of nothing and nowhere, and only so intangible as they were could they lay claim to so intangible a thing. And so they did.

The wind dried them on the walk home. By the time they got to Eccleston's back fence all the joking had stopped. They had given in to tiredness and in tiredness to silence. Grey left the other three on their way to Eccleston's house.

He climbed through the rusted barbwire and his father's red bitch ran to his heel. She licked the creek off his shins and licked his canvas boots. The back door was unlocked and the windows were all open. He crept through the kitchen, careful not to wake his sister.

She sat awake before the Black Madonna and icon lamp. The tips of her fingers touched the glass.

She smiled. She did not care that he was late, only that finally he had come.

THEY WERE BOTH happy. It was deep summer and the long days barely passed; they were spent in a state of staid, balmy dreaming that was not real. There was nothing else to do tonight, nor all tomorrow. Grey's next shift at Bizzell's was three days away. His cold muscles were tired and gently aching from pushing against the current at the creek.

He showered and fell asleep beside his sister on their lounge chair, a cool wind from the mountains playing with the ragged veils of curtains in the living room.

# II

GREY TOOK HIS 1958 FC HOLDEN TO COLLECT HIS SISTER from school. A storm moved swiftly across the plain. Nine inches of rain had fallen already that month and the season's leafy green sorghum was spread across the land. The sorghum pushed hard against rotting wooden gates at the roadside. Telephone lines sagged as though burdened by the weight of the enormous bruising sky. Leaves sailed to the ground through shafts of golden light, borne upon the storm wind.

There was a bang like a rifle going off and the truck tilted. He had blown a tyre. He pulled off the road. He took his jack from the boot but realized he had leant his wheel brace to Matt Thiebaud. The sky began to drizzle. Then it was pouring. He sheltered at the back of the corrugated-iron Windmill Fruit Market. He took a dark-brown cigarette from a crushed box in the pocket of his jeans and reshaped it. He leant on a pile of blue crates with his back to the highway and smoked and watched the storm empty on sorghum and barley stubble.

When the best of the storm was passed he put the cigarette under his heel and set out walking.

SHE HAD WALKED along Banjalang Street in the rain while the town children ran for shelter. She crossed the box girder at the edge of town. Her hair was stuck to her face when he met her on the brink of the highway proper. The colour of her hair seemed like it should run like dye into her pale cold face. Her dirty, ill-fitting clothes clung to her bones.

She sighed deeply.

"I'm sorry," he said.

She took his arm.

SHE FELL BEHIND him. She pulled flowers from the Natal grass that grew along the edge of the highway and her hair blew about her face in the north wind. Dark-blue cloud was banked in the northeastern distance and lightning flashed and made the cloud a lantern. They met Grey's truck and Irene stood by, watching the road and the rippling grass and the flashing clouds while Grey borrowed a wheel brace from an old ringer at the fruit market and changed the tyre.

A WOMAN WITH richly-dyed mauve hair and a swollen red face came charging out of their house when Grey and Irene were on the stairs.

"The restaurant opened twenty minutes ago," said Angela Teal, tying her hair and scampering past them on her way to a night's waitressing.

Grey stared out his bedroom window onto the rain-drenched country. The words "You must always look after me" came like pencils of light from that immense emptiness. And he turned and saw she who had spoken them, standing in his doorway having showered and put on dry clothes. She came to his bed and knelt beside him and looked out the window. Grey smiled and patted down her hair. Then Irene smiled too.

THEY SAT BY the window eating melon cooled in an icebox and watching the claw of another northern storm grip the house.

The rain spattered hard on their iron roof and they shouted to be heard above it. The storm swept in gusts across the plain and emptied itself in wild flourishes across the green undulations that Grey would always call Eccleston's, whoever held the deed. The rain flooded the gutters and soaked the veranda.

By half-past five the storm was spent and left gilded clouds in its wake.

Through the window Grey saw the houseyard was overrun with milk thistle and buffel grass. The white flowers of a lemon tree fell on the wasted fruit of fourteen winters. Honeysuckle and cat's claw contended with the wild jasmine for dominance over the jangling fences. Paddymelon vine overran what were once garden beds. These domestic things that had grown wild belonged to the gently-eroding memory of Grey's mother.

There were few things left on earth that recalled the first Irene North.

Her daughter rarely asked about her. Even the copper-tinged photographs Grey gave her were afforded no special place in her room. They were left in drawers and never viewed. The first Irene's piano sat idly in the corner of the living room. Her daughter was too flighty to ever seriously sit down to it, and there was no one to teach her and, as she protested, the hammers and strings had decayed and only a few keys either side of middle C were not dead or hopelessly out of tune. Very rarely she played a melancholy melody of her own making on the white keys, a melody that recalled the old church music Grey heard late at night on the radio, attached to strange foreign names like Léonin and Josquin.

Grey kept a single, favourite photograph of his mother, sometimes in his wallet, sometimes in his bedroom drawer or the glovebox of his truck. Occasionally he would sit on his bed on a golden afternoon such as this, in quiet contemplation of the girl smiling out of his barely-remembered past, smiling that eyes-closed-into-crescents smile that made her irresistible. In the photograph she was standing with his father, newly married, in a cheap cotton dress and fleece-lined pink corduroy coat against the winter, looking every bit the child she was. The picture was taken six months before Grey's birth. He tried to recognize his mother's face.

Better than her face now he recalled her voice. Inconsequential phrases came most often to mind, these rather than what should have been the significant things she had said to him: worldly advice, declarations of love ... Those must have been spoken, but were all forgotten. He remembered such things as a passing comment about his dirty hair, or a simple condescending joke of the kind that is shared between a mother and child ... He remembered one winter afternoon when he had run off after school and not made it home until after dark. He had been lost in the woods. He did not yet know to follow the dry creeks and he had cried, not for fear but because his mother would be upset. At last he found his way home. Irene had searched the woods on the creek then returned to the house in case he was there. She had been about to set out in the dark when she heard his steps on the stairs. "It's me," he whimpered when he opened the back door. His mother wiped her tears and held him and smiled: "I know who you are, little boy."

GREY AND HIS sister went to a wrought-iron bench beneath the stringybark in the yard. He dried the bench with an old shirt and they sat down. He rolled and lit a cigarette. Insects rose out of the grass into the golden light that clung fast to the trees and even to the air. The washed air meant a cool night. He did not want to go back inside. He was avoiding their father who would drink very gently and quietly by himself on his days off the railways now, drinking cheap whisky while Angela was at work or visited relatives in the city. Now that the rain had stopped, the man's heavy presence could be felt within the walls, and Grey was eager for the energy of Eccleston and the boys. Mahony's Boxing Troupe was in town tonight and Eccleston would fight.

"Please take me along."

"It's no good for you."

But he did not want to leave her alone.

He went inside to tell his father they were going, and the man who was staring out his window and descending fast into the inarticulate final stage of afternoon drunkenness nodded and asked no questions.

# III

HALFWAY TO TOWN WAS SOLITARY HILL AND THE DRIVE-
in movies, and Irene knelt backwards in the seat of Grey's truck
to see the Friday night reel alight.

"Can't we go to the pictures?"

"Maybe later. Let's see the fights first."

"But I don't like fights."

"You said you wanted to come."

She sighed.

"After the fights we'll do something else," Grey said.

"See the pictures?"

"Maybe."

"Why maybe?"

"You don't even watch them. You just fall asleep."

She laughed. On another night she would not be dragged
to the pictures.

"So we'll go?"

"Maybe."

THE BOXING TROUPE was set on an empty dirt lot behind the
Railway Hotel. The scattered crowd only half-filled the lot. Grey
picked out Matt Thiebaud, Raughrie Norman and Hart Bates.
Bates was the younger brother of Rod Bates, the boy Eccleston
fought on the night of the fires fourteen-years ago. He had taken
to tagging along with Raughrie Norman since Norman began

spending three days a week shovelling sawdust at the sawmill for a little less than a living.

Mahony banged his bass drum and called the last of his fighters up to the scaffold where Eccleston already stood beside a shirtless raw-boned boy in jeans. On the other side of the boy was a pot-bellied gas worker who looked more than sixty. Standing beside the challengers were Mahony's fighters: a young Italian-looking boy; a toothless Aborigine of indeterminable age, who Mahony said had lost his last six fights; and a short, heavily muscled man with grey temples and tattoos that ran the lengths of his arms.

Grey put his arm around Irene's shoulders and pressed through the loose gathering. Eccleston winked at Irene from the scaffold and she gave him a half-hearted, nervous smile.

Inside the tent the crowd of high-school kids and district farm boys pushed hard up beside a thick rope that made a circle on the dirt. The rope would be the ring and the crowd the ropes. Irene held Grey's hand tight as he pushed them into a good enough position to see Eccleston fight but not so close as to be dangerous. Often enough at these shows people in the front row were punched squarely in the face or trodden or fallen on.

"Can you see?"

"Yes," she answered, but the light had gone out of her face.

Once in the ring, the same toothless black troupe fighter who on the scaffold had been on a six-fight losing streak Mahony announced as having won his last twelve by knockout. The silver-haired conman smiled and blew the whistle for the bout. The crowd howled as the toothless black fighter danced around the pot-bellied old man and did not throw a punch. The old man stood square and made circles with his gloves. The troupe fighter threw a haymaker that was intended to miss, and the crowd whistled and howled. He ducked the first serious punch of the bout and came inside with a quick combination, slamming the old man's face and then stomach. The old man grimaced and bent over to let blood run from his nose and rubbed his belly with his gloves. Mahony sneered. He did not like the fights to finish too soon. He spoke in his fighter's ear. The old man shaped up again. Despite his lowered guard, the old man took a blow to the kidneys that was not meant to hurt him, yet he fell to his knees. The crowd jeered but the old man did not get up. He looked very sick this time. Grey looked down at his sister who was no longer watching the ring.

"I don't like these people."

She spoke just loud enough beneath the crowd for him to hear.

"All right," he said, and he knew he had been a fool to bring her. "We'll just stay to watch Ook."

There was an emaciated official whose job it was to glove the local fighters, but Eccleston's gloves were tied in a corner of the tent by Matt Thiebaud. Thiebaud pulled the gloves tight and got Eccleston to squeeze and open his hand while Raughrie Norman stood by to no purpose. Grey caught his sister peeking back through the bodies of the crowd at the broad-shouldered boy she knew well but who seemed strange to her now, slamming his gloved fists together and looking fiercely ring-ward.

The Italian-looking boy that Mahony called Kid Valentine limbered up in the human ring, eyes gleaming with hollow confidence. But Eccleston would not be rushed. When his gloves were tied the fight began.

Eccleston pushed hard and close into Kid Valentine's body so the boy could not get a decent punch off and was forced to wheel back to regain his reach. With the boy unsteady on his back foot, Eccleston threw a short left hook into his mouth then hit him with his favoured right and blood flew into the air and onto the dirt and the troupe fighter fell into the crowd on his back. Grey felt a pull on his shirt and Irene looked up at him with confused and teary eyes.

"All right," he said.

THEY WENT TO the town's café and shared a toasted cheese sandwich and an iced coffee. In a while Grey saw Eccleston come onto the street with the boys slapping him on the back and smiling. Twenty dollars a minute and three three-minute rounds. He had earned a decent purse for the night. Grey knew the boys would go to one or other of the bigger district towns now to squander the better part of the money between them. Eccleston looked around on the street for him. Grey did not call out. Eccleston had seen Irene was with him and would understand.

HE PARKED THE truck by the back fence and they walked to Lake Wivenhoe.

He did not expect to find the boys at the lake. He thought they would already be gone. By the time he was aware of them it was too late to turn back.

"Where were you this afternoon?' Thiebaud called.

"I was there. I left early. Where's Ook?"

"He's comin later. He had somethin or other to do with Pos. The whisky run, probably."

"Easy win?"

"Not so easy in the end. He had some fight in him, that bastard."

Grey sat down on a hessian sack and Irene sat beside him. Wisps of red cloud drifted under a frayed grey blanket like loosed flares. Drowned eucalypts stood in the shallows of the lake and the rippling water slapped against them. Then the red clouds turned white and were shredded by the wind and the boys sat in a deep blue dusk.

"She go with you everywhere?' said Hart Bates, leaning back with a bottle of beer.

Grey glanced at his sister. She tried not to look embarrassed. He glared at Bates and the boy turned away and hurled a stone into the lake. Bates said something under his breath to Raughrie Norman. It was not a great insult – only that there was no point carting around girls who were not good for the one thing girls were good for. Still, Raughrie Norman shook his head and refused to answer.

Thiebaud threw an empty beer bottle that struck Bates on the shoulder. He talked through his cigarette.

"Hart, if you weren't so clever as you are, you'd be an idiot."

"Lucky for me."

"Real lucky."

Grey smiled reassurance at his sister. He asked the boys where they were going.

"Toogoolawah, Crows Nest, Villeneuve," Thiebaud said. "We'll see when Ook gets here. You comin?"

"I think I'll stay home."

He knew Irene would not go back to the restaurant now, even if Amy was working.

Grey stood and said that they had things to do. Thiebaud reached up to loosely shake Grey's hand and said he would see him tomorrow.

They walked back toward the house.

A bulky figure with a bushel cornsack rolled up on his shoulder appeared out of the blue dark. Another body came behind, scrawny and black like one of the scrub trees in the flat country to the west.

Eccleston said he had been at Grey's house. Grey said the boys were still waiting. Eccleston talked through his smoke and asked if Grey was coming out with them tonight and Grey shook his head. Eccleston mussed Irene's hair.

"You're going to Toogoolawah."

"Reckon so. Came into some money. You saw the fight?"

"I saw part of it. You feel all right?"

"Yeah."

"What about the other boy?"

"He's all right."

The old black man trailing Eccleston was Possum Gallanani. After Eccleston returned from Borallon, Possum continued the education begun by the boy's father. He taught Eccleston how to break horses and how to track brumbies by the marks they made with their teeth in trees, and he and the boy worked for three months taking colts and fillies out of the Carnarvon Gorge and turning them into saddle horses – stealing cattle that had escaped into the national park meanwhile. But "No jobs now for old blackfella," Possum would say. And it was true. He did not have the know-how to apply for a social security check. He did not have a bank account. He could neither read nor write. He lived off money from a scant few jobs for August Tanner and from his illegal whisky run.

"What's up with Pos?"

Eccleston smiled.

The old man whimpered and clutched his behind.

"He got shot with salt pellets," Eccleston said, "cuttin home across Tanner's northwest country from my place."

"Just now?"

"Just now."

"What were you up to, Pos?"

Possum grunted with disgust. Eccleston spoke for him.

"He was usin my keg to make his whisky, then was sneakin it back home in the dark."

Many old men of the country made their own drink, but a black man carrying homemade liquor along the highway at night was a needless temptation to offer already bored police. So the clandestine route.

"Why the hell would Tanner have reason to shoot?' Grey said.

"He reckons someone's been strippin the heads off his milo for birdseed. The old bastard's been sittin out there in the afternoons watchin for his thief."

"Pos?"

"Yep. But he doesn't use it for birdseed. He mashes it up and eats it himself."

Possum gave another groan of pain.

"He'll be all right," Eccleston said. "I've been hit with those things before."

He said they had already taken out the pellets with tweezers. The word "tweezers' drew a wail from the old Aborigine.

"I was on the fuggin creek," he said. "Tanner yells at me the creek's the Queen's land. I said to im, I never seen er walkin it!"

The boys laughed.

"The Queen's too busy cartin whisky up and down creeks in England," said Eccleston. "And anyway, you don't know how to walk this country, old man, that's why you ended up shot."

"I can walk anywhere within a thousand miles a ere. When I'm sober. Before me eyes went bad, I could."

It was true that a film of sun-induced cataracts lay over the old man's red eyes.

Eccleston smiled.

"You went to the house?' said Grey.

"That's right."

"How was Bill?"

He shrugged and Grey nodded. It was a hopeless hope – that he might have been able to leave Irene at home after all.

They left Eccleston and Possum on their way to the lake. The lights of cars leaving town banded the western dark.

IRENE CLIMBED ONTO the round bonnet of her brother's truck and Grey told her to wait for him there. The sky was blown clean of cloud now and the firmament hung over them in full gleaming array. Irene lay back on the windscreen.

She could name much of the night sky – Sirius and Canopus and Rigel and Betelgeuse, which she called "belting geese', and the lesser stars too, all at a glance. She took the names from a survey of astronomy that her mother had used at school. She knew to the night and to the hour what would rise. She quizzed Grey on which luminaries were which – which were stars and which were planets – but his eyes were not strong enough to see the absence of flicker in the planets and it was a game she always won.

Inside the house their father was asleep. Grey wrote a note and put it under the bedside lamp. He changed his shirt and wet his face and hair and came back outside.

Irene told him there was going to be a meteor shower tonight, the Alpha Centaurids. Sister Charbel had said so at school. But so far she had seen nothing.

"Let's go for a drive," Grey said.

Irene jumped off the bonnet and landed awkwardly on her feet.

"Where are we going?"

"Around."

"To the pictures?"

"There's most likely nothing on."

"Where then? Vanessa's?"

"Why not?"

"Can't we do something else?"

"What's wrong with Vanessa?"

"Nothing, I spose."

But for the second time in the night the light had gone out of her eyes.

# IV

IRENE HARDLY SPOKE ON THE DRIVE. SHE WITHDREW
out the window into the night sky. It was remarkable, Grey
thought, that such an excitable girl could become so pensive.
It was a trait of hers that at times seemed whimsical, but it was
not insincere. She was a fourteen-year-old girl capable of
genuine melancholy, that was not easily relieved once it came.

He put his hand on her shoulder and she turned from the
window and smiled sadly and her eyes were like dark ponds in
her odd little face. She relaxed back into the wistful expression
that was hers in repose. The tops of her ears protruded through
her unwashed hair. Her splotchy complexion and watery eyes
ever made her appear as though she had just finished crying. She
is not pretty, Grey thought. Her face was too strange to meet
any standard of prettiness – yet her face was affecting. A small
ache came into his heart whenever she was sad.

ON HIGHWAY 54 they rolled through darkness broken by glints
of wet sorghum and the veranda lights of farm houses on stilts.
Plump women in flapping cotton dresses stood watching the night
from the stairs of the houses. Horses leant over wire fences and
picked at the feed on the roadside.

But there were tracts that threatened the country's peace.
The foundations of a shopping centre were being laid fifteen
kilometres west of the Brisbane Valley turn-off. Bulldozers and
rollers that would broaden the highway sat in ditches off the

asphalt. More machines sat atop the dirt walls of enormous dams. Patches of biscuit-cutter houses appeared. The houses were set on new and overlit roads that ran circuitous routes, else to dead ends, like mazes in the backs of cheap magazines. And all the houses seemed empty. Towns were bypassed with only reflective road signs to indicate them: names and arrows pointing somewhere out into the banks of depthless black begotten by the highway radiance. But the names came to signify nothing. The places they called upon were no longer discrete.

WHEN THEY CAME into Haigslea the land opened up. The sprawl did not reach so far. The lights of houses trickled and pooled across the valley like water. Orange lamps picked out railway crossings and desultory children on bicycles lingering about the line.

Grey and Irene stopped at the high roadside pie stand called the Pieteria and bought a packet of cigarettes and two small bottles of ginger beer. Beside the Pieteria was a roadhouse hotel called the Sundowner. Across the asphalt was a big Moreton Bay fig and a paint-stripped house and a blue school bus that had not been driven in twenty years. Then the land fell hard down into the valley and in the distance was the blue ridge of the D'Aguilar Range.

Grey placed a bottle of ginger beer in Irene's hand. She stared at it.

"You go on if you want."

"What do you mean?"

"You go on to Vanessa's. I'll wait here. Ask the lady what time she closes."

"I'm not leaving you."

Grey uncapped his sister's bottle with his pocket-knife and the over-carbonated drink spilled onto his hands. She was looking at her shoes. Grey sighed.

"If you didn't want to come you should have said so earlier."

"I did," she whispered.

He sighed.

"Don't you have some friends I could leave you with?"

Directly he spoke he was sorry.

"You're my only friend," she lied.

"Come on, we won't stay long. We'll get something to eat with Vanessa and head back."

She dragged her feet toward the truck.

THEY DROVE OVER the railway tracks into a wide street and stopped in front of a house built of stone.

A plumed middle-aged woman opened the door to him.

"Hello, Mrs Humphries. Is Vanessa in?"

"Grey. It's … it's nice to see you again. And this, of course, is your sister."

"Yes. This is Irene."

"Well," said Mrs Humphries, and her eyes darted between Grey and his sister, unsure what to say next. "Well, you've grown up since last I saw you, miss."

Irene nodded indifferently.

Vanessa's mother always received Grey with fraudulent welcome. He forgave her for it. There were plenty of reasons why a twenty-four-year-old weekday-night service station attendant was not an ideal choice to have calling on your daughter, and Grey was sympathetic. Probably she had heard too that his friends were reckless, and that half-truth made the fact of him even more difficult on the woman's middle-class conscience.

"Vanessa!' she called in a voice that contained strains of warning and reprimand at once. She did not wait long enough for a reply before she went to get her daughter, to afford her one last moment alone with the girl and make certain the strictures of her leaving the house. She left Grey and Irene standing on the doorstep.

A pretty, sandy-blonde girl appeared at the end of the corridor.

"Well," she said, "look who's here!"

"Thought I'd come by and see if you were doing anything."

"Hardly. Hey, Irene."

Irene whimpered a reply. Vanessa pulled on a pair of sandshoes.

"Isn't your brother handsome," she said when she came out the door and took his hand.

Irene looked up.

"I don't think so."

Vanessa's mother tried to intervene, to impress one last order upon her daughter, but they were already down the stairs.

"THAT'S IF I really go," said Vanessa. "But I suppose I will go. You can't stay at home forever, can you?"

"No," Grey said.

They were talking about an offer of work at a legal office in Brisbane at the end of the year. All young people left for the city eventually.

They had only gone as far as that same pie stand at the turn-off to town. The pie stand and the Sundowner Hotel beside it were the only places open at this time of night. Vanessa could not stay out late, so there was no point in driving to find something better. The highway was long and this far west entertainment was not one of its concerns. After the Sundowner you would drive an hour before you found a cup of instant coffee at anywhere other than a service station.

The smell of wet crops carried along the road with a wind from the southwest.

"I'll be finished at the end of the year," Vanessa said. "I guess I'd like some time off after that, but then, I'd be a fool not to consider it."

Grey only half-listened. He was trying to remember how long he had chased this girl. Like most young people of the district they were acquainted early. They had kissed once as teenagers. But it was five years before she noticed him again: that night he found her right here, sitting crying under a highway lamp after a run-in with a drunken boy at the Sundowner. He had asked if she wanted to be driven home. Back then she lived closer to him: at Fernvale, the next town south along the Valley Highway. She was called the prettiest girl in the district. Her sensual figure, sun-bleached hair and olive skin suggested vibrant health. And her habit – whether deliberate, he did not know – of unexpectedly touching boys' arms when they were near her enhanced her charms. Grey put the habit down to a need to be constantly loved and considered. That feeling was so foreign to him that he did not regard it as a flaw. It made him smile. She was not self-possessed, though some mistook her gestures for self-possession. Her deepest desire was to be possessed by another. He discovered she was incapable of achieving a boast. Try as she might, even a comment on her own desirability sounded like the unartful, uncertain plea of a child to have an adult notice something special about them.

But they lived in different towns. She was flighty. She stayed in the city through the university year and she had difficult parents. All the boys of the district but Grey had long ago given up on her. Though he was her favourite among the boys west of the mountains, they were not quite involved in a romance. He wondered what she got up to in the city. She assured him he was her favourite here and everywhere else.

A sedan screamed past on the highway and broke his meditation. Vanessa's eyes brightened.

"Did you hear about the man who was killed here last week?"

"Only that much."

Grey had read it in the paper. The man was killed when his car was shouldered off the road by another vehicle and smashed in a ditch. People who had heard the crash suggested shots had been fired, but that was not proven; it may have been tyres blowing. There was no mention in the newspaper report of who the man was or where he was going or coming from; no mention of what motive his attackers might have acted on – if they were attackers. Likely the motives were unknown. It was as though these things were inessential to the event that belonged to the highway alone: a place where destinations and purposes were irrelevant, where random accidents were the way of things. A place as violent as it was dull and forgettable. Only the departure speed of the vehicle, the location it left the road, and the possibility of two shots being fired were recorded.

"They're gone now," said Vanessa of the possible attackers. She indicated the highway west with a flick of her hand, as though any search for them beyond this point must be futile. "You can't help but wonder who's driving around."

Grey had not noticed Irene go off by herself and sit down on the side stairs of the Sundowner. She held her chin in her hands and stared across the highway. She was staring at horses that stood sleeping beside the bus. The mountains behind the horses were lost to the dark.

"Poor kid," said Vanessa.

Only then did Grey realise she was not with them. He felt a regrettable relief at not having her in his shadow for the moment. "She acts a little strange though, you must admit. She's so quiet."

"She has no mother – or father," Grey justified.

"I heard what one of her schoolmates said to her the other day. What was it … ?' Vanessa had heard because Grey had told her and he did not feel like hearing it again. "If he had a dog that poor he'd give it away," she answered herself. "Boys are so awful."

In fact what had been said was much worse than that.

"Do you think it upset her very much? She seems the kind of girl who could get used to it."

Grey looked up from his steak pie. Whatever Irene was, she was not a "kind'. He wanted to say her whims were all her own. And the idea of her being teased at school upset him greatly. He had gone to the boy's father's house and demanded the man make his son apologize.

"What's wrong?' Vanessa asked him.

The look on her face showed she had meant nothing at all

by what she said. There was never any malice in her words, however ill-chosen.

Grey smiled.

Vanessa loved to talk and Grey was sure it was simply the sound of her own voice that gratified her. He liked the sound of it too and was content to listen. It was a voice that, despite a few trivial, personal insecurities, was certain of the shape of the world. In Vanessa's conversation, misfortune only possessed the power to affect other people, people beyond her circle. A voice made by the big stone house and mahogany furniture and land-scaped gardens as surely as the plains once shaped the language of aborigines. She was habitually happy and had a precious gift for making those around her happy too. She seemed aglow with the life that was promised her, and Grey's heart lightened. Her upbringing and all the circumstances of her life were so different to his own. He held her hand across the table.

"What will I do when you move away for good?' he said.

"Marry one of the Blandford girls in Mary Smokes," she teased. "I hear Anne and Eve are already gone, so you should start on Libby. You won't miss me."

"And if I do?"

"How could I tie myself to someone like you? You've been in jail!"

"The Toogoolawah lockup isn't jail," Grey smiled. "And it wasn't my fault that put me there. What would you do if someone you didn't know walked straight up to the bar you were sitting at and hit you?"

"Fall down and cry."

"Well that's what I did, and I still ended up in trouble."

"What happened really?' Vanessa grinned.

"A bloke questioned the femininity of a girl I was with, but she was too drunk to fight anymore that night so I had to step in."

"You fool. You're never serious with me. But really, that's a terrible story – if it's even partly true. And after that I suppose you learnt your lesson about Toogoolawah girls and came running after me."

Grey smiled and then looked past Vanessa and met his sister's sad eyes. She turned away and resumed staring at the horses. He sighed.

"I should go."

"But you never come see me. And in a couple of weeks I'll be gone again!"

"I'll make it up to you," he winked.

"But we just got here! And I don't mean that, you vulgar hick. Any wonder it scares my mother when I tell her the things you say." And she giggled.

Grey looked inside the remodelled van. The pie lady was leaning over the counter staring at them, no doubt wanting to close. He and Vanessa had finished eating, and Irene's half-eaten blueberry pie was cold.

"Don't you have to be home?"

"Not so early. Stay a little while longer. Give Irene a couple of dollars to buy a milkshake and we'll go for a drive. Or, at least, the bottle shop at the Sundowner is still open. Let's get a seven-fifty of whisky. We can all drink it sitting in the field."

"A capful of whisky will put Irene to sleep."

"Well, that's not so bad. The grass is soft behind here – for lying and looking at the stars," she teased. "See! I can be bad too."

Did she really think of him in that light? If so, how little she understood him. He could have been a child of respectability just as well as her. He looked again at Irene, sitting on the hotel stairs and staring at the sky, and thought how he was not half as wild as his sister.

Vanessa had been promised entertainment for the night and then disappointed. It was only a quarter to ten. But Grey was tired of the teasing that would lead nowhere tonight.

"I'm sorry. I should take Irene home. It doesn't look like she's having much fun."

"Well, she's not the only one."

Grey looked into Vanessa's sham indignant eyes and entreated sympathy.

She sighed then stood up from the table.

"Come on then."

HE DROPPED VANESSA off in front of her house and drove back onto the highway. The highway was even emptier and lonelier than before. The distant lights of farmer's houses had gone out. The bulky women in flapping dresses had retreated inside. The wind blustered through the wound-down windows of the truck and was almost cold and on the straight road Irene began to cry.

"What's wrong?"

"Nothing."

"You can tell me, Irene. You can tell me anything."

"It's nothing, Grey. Really, it's nothing."

He furrowed his brow and tried to make light of it, whatever it was, by affecting a sombre face. She wiped her eyes with her dress, revealing all of her thin legs, and he was moved by her innocence. He put his hand on the back of her head to comfort her.

"Don't, Grey. Please just drive. Girls can't help crying sometimes. Don't you know that?"

"All right," he whispered. He rested his elbow on the windowsill. "All right."

She lay on his shoulder and fell asleep, bouncing awake at each flaw in the road. He left her sleeping in the truck when he stopped at lonely Rusty's Roadhouse to refuel.

She lay down with her legs curled up on the vinyl seat and slept there until home.

When they reached Solitary Hill the night's final movie was playing. In the last hour of the show the ticket seller abandoned his booth and you could drive in and watch for free.

The only parks taken on the lot were just back of centre. Grey pulled the truck up at the eastern edge where they were all alone. Irene woke when the engine stopped. She looked up at the movie screen and smiled and returned to sleep. Grey did not hang the speaker in the window, nor try to follow the movie. He watched the play of light on the screen and felt the west wind flush on his cheek.

When he woke the dozen cars that had sat before the screen were filing out through the gates. Irene was asleep in his lap. He ran his fingers through her hair.

"You poor child," he whispered. "I'll always be with you. I promise."

They were the last car on the lot. Soon the attendant would be bolting shut the gates. Grey felt like sitting a while longer. He sighed and held her arm until she sat up and looked all around, trying to remember where she was.

On the short run home she leant on her arm on the window. He thought she was asleep again when she cried out to him.

"Grey, stop the car! I saw a meteor."

"What did it look like?"

"Like a shooting star, only green and much brighter. Grey, stop!"

They pulled onto the side of the road and he saw a bright green flash that came blazing in seconds across a thousand miles. They climbed into the tray and lay down on hessian sacks and watched the night sky kindled with ancient rocks.

When the meteors failed she spoke, genuinely happy for the first time in the night:

"The next time we see a shower like that we'll be a thousand years old."

# V

THE MORNING WAS CRISP AND CLEAN AND THE COUNTRY
was tinged the colour of lemons. Six blue-roan two-year-olds
stood in the water yard and Tanner and Grey isolated one and ran
it into the roundyard where Eccleston had wrapped his cotton
rope around the top rail.

The filly held her head high and her ears back. She skirted
the rails and blew mucous from flared nostrils. Tanner turned
to Eccleston.

"Even that black uncle a yours would've had a job to break
this lot. Had he shown up, that is."

Eccleston only shrugged. He did not know where Possum
was.

The horse had been pacing the opposite end of the yard to
where Tanner and Grey sat on the top rail, but when Eccleston
moved into the centre it stood still and square to him.

He stared into the horse's eyes and flicked at its heels with
a length of rope, hunting it around the edge of the yard. He
kept the horse circling until it dropped its head. He tossed a loop
around its neck and stood at the horse's shoulder and pulled
gently on the rope until the horse turned and faced him, and he
immediately released the pressure. Then he changed his angle
to the horse, changed it a dozen times, always bringing the filly's
head toward him and releasing the rope when she turned, and
always drawing a little closer. And all the while he spoke to the
horse, impressing upon it the calm tone of his voice. He drew

close enough to take off the loop, then threw the rope at the horse's heels again. Then he walked in front of the horse and turned his left shoulder and dropped his eyes and the horse came toward him. He walked away and the horse followed.

He scratched the filly's forehead. She sniffed at his face.

He scratched the horse's shoulder and then leant on its neck. He scratched its flanks with a length of yellow poly Grey handed him. He got Grey to bring him a halter. He slung his rope over the horse's neck and slid the halter over its nose, but when the crownpiece touched its ears the horse broke away.

The horse stood at the opposite end of the yard.

Eccleston tried the halter twice more, and twice the horse broke from him.

"I'm not payin you by the hour," said Tanner. "I want these done tomorrow."

Eccleston eyed the man on the top rail.

"Six green horses in two days?"

"I did six a day when I was your age."

"I bet they were good too!"

Tanner shrugged and spat off the rails.

"Tie her up and put a saddle on her."

"How none a your clients never shot you is a mystery to me, old man?"

In the days when Tanner broke horses it was common enough to drive past this yard and see a horse tied with a foot of slack to a post, the man throwing a tin under the horse's feet – else pulling it down and beating it with a burlap sack – for mysterious purposes he called, 'gettin it used to bein bossed'.

Tanner climbed off the rail and put his hands on Eccleston's saddle.

"Not yet," said Eccleston. "You know I ride em bareback first."

Eccleston took his ragged old saddle and tack and set it down in the yard with the other horses to let them nip and paw at it.

Eccleston spoke to Grey.

"Guess I'm doin it the old blackfella way."

"How's that?"

"Rope em and tie em to snubbin posts. Pull em into the race, then ride em out till they get sick a throwin me off."

"It's faster," said Tanner.

"It's not."

"Whose horses are they?' Tanner snorted.

Eccleston spat.

"I'm gettin her to lead before I do anything," he said.

"Suit yourself. Just as long as they're done tomorrow night."

Eccleston slung his rope over a rail and pressed rosin into the palm of a glove and pulled the rosin into the rope. He picked up a loop and took up the slack in his left hand. He threw the loop that fell over the filly's ears and onto her shoulders. The rope pulled tight around her neck. He dug his heels in the dirt and held the filly until she was still. He drew along the rope but the horse reared and ran at him, shying away at the last, pulling him over and the rope out of his hand. The horse pranced about the end of the yard, as skittish as it had been in the beginning, head high and wary, now dragging the rope.

Eccleston collected his angler's hat and brushed and reshaped it. Grey ran him a cup of water from their esky that sat atop a post.

"That thing was sired by a goat!' said Eccleston.

"The blood's all right," said Tanner. "We had some of these horses here last year. She's full a grain, that's all. Her guts are burnin."

Eccleston looked at Grey then back at Tanner who looked up at the sky.

"The bloke I bought em off just inherited the string. He's a boy. He thinks it makes em more saleable if their coats are shinin."

"When did they get off the truck?"

"Last night."

Eccleston began untying his glove.

"Leave em in the yard for a day with water, no feed. I'll come back tomorrow afternoon and saddle em out. The day after that I'll break em."

"No can do. I've already got a buyer. I promised em delivered broken this week."

"How far away does your bloke live?"

"On the border. Near Goondiwindi."

"Well, I'll start em tomorrow. A truck can get to the border in a day."

"Ideally," Tanner said.

"Ideally what?"

"Ideally, you could start em tomorrow. Only, I've got business in the city day after tomorrow."

"No matter," said Eccleston. "I've got nothin else on."

"Clients don't like the idea a boys bein on the place when I'm not around. The horses here are my responsibility, you understand."

"No. But they're your horses – in a manner of speakin."

"I'll do half," said Grey, jumping down off the rail. "So you don't have to get thrown off all six. Three solid meals of dirt are enough for any man in one day." He looked up at Tanner. "Full-pay again. Me and him'll split it. All right?"

"Can you break a horse?"

"You want em done in two days?"

Tanner spat.

"All right then."

Eccleston turned to Tanner.

"You still got that old white mare here?"

"She's in the willow paddock."

"Go and catch her for me, Grey. There's a bridle and rein in the back of the truck. Ride her back. We'll quieten em down easier with her in the yard."

When Grey left to get the mare, a late model sedan neither he nor Eccleston recognized pulled up the drive. The man who got out wore a suede jacket and sunglasses. His thinning brown hair was oiled firmly back on his skull.

Tanner climbed off the rail.

"If your useless black uncle shows up while I'm inside, tell him he's not gettin a red cent."

Eccleston stopped working the filly and spat and took a rolled cigarette from his shirt pocket and sucked on the end.

"You fire another shot at him, old man, and you'll regret it."

Tanner was suddenly nervous. He turned to the man beside him and mumbled something and the two of them laughed.

"Don't set fire to the place while I'm inside, Ook. The bloke I'm sellin the horses to cares about presentation. He won't want em ripped apart goin over fences."

Tanner drove the man the quarter-mile from the yards to his house.

"Who's that?' said Grey when he returned with the mare.

Eccleston shrugged.

"Looks like a racetrack urger or ex-cop."

THEY WERE TOO tired to speak when they got into Grey's truck late that afternoon. They splashed iodine on their shoulders and forearms that were wounded from being thrown into the yard rails. Lightning flashed on every horizon and a cloud as black as charred wood pulled wispy orange tendrils beneath it.

Tanner and the man who had visited him came back to the yards. The man got in his car and drove away.

Tanner leant in Eccleston's window.

"After tomorrow you've worked your last bloody day for me, you ungrateful black bastard."

"Is that right?"

Tanner had spoken words akin to these at least a dozen times before.

"Don't you ever talk to me like that in front of another man, you hear?"

"Like what?"

"Threaten me like you did about Pos."

"Settle down," Grey said.

"Do you hear me?"

"Settle the hell down," Grey said again. "Who was that bloke, anyway?"

"He takes bets."

"What on?"

"Whatever you like. He'll give you odds. I met him at a card game in– Well, at a card game."

"In a hotel at Dinmore," said Eccleston.

Dinmore was a nowhere suburb west of the city. It was little more than a stinking abattoir and industrial sheds. Eccleston had only guessed; it was one of only two semi-permanent card games he knew. But he saw by the look on Tanner's face that he had guessed right.

"I wouldn't tell you unless you wanted to play," said Tanner.

Eccleston laughed.

"Do you get a finder's fee for the poor suckers you bring to the table?"

"The man's my friend."

"Your *friend*," Eccleston grinned. "So you're mates with a proper moonlight state man now. You must be happy."

Tanner did not reply.

Eccleston had been once to the clean and characterless bar at Dinmore and seen men dressed in cheap casual wear climb the stairs to a room where they played blackjack, else roulette on a fold-out backgammon board. The set up was childish, but the amounts of money staked were not. The game had driven one man to suicide. So it was said. The men who gambled at the bar were out-of-towners. No one lived at Dinmore. Some came from the Brisbane Valley and further west – truck drivers, gas workers and meatworks buyers – and some were from the city. Some had been local landholders and some were pious Pentecostals who oscillated between vice and piety and, depending on the week, might be present at the table, else preaching about the evils of such practice in one or other of the shopping-mart churches on the outskirts. Certain bored landholders west of Brisbane had become wealthy by associations made at the table in Dinmore. Men whose country had always been too stony or sour or timbered to run cattle began buying out neighbours.

From the bar at the Dinmore Hotel you heard the occasional table thumped upstairs and a glass smash on the floorboards, perhaps a raised voice. But finally there was quiet. And the bartender would avoid the eyes of certain men who came down the stairs.

And apparently Tanner had linked himself with at least one of these men.

"What do you have to do with him?' Grey asked.

Tanner took a swig of whisky from the flask he kept always in his jeans.

"He wants me to introduce him to horse breedin. Buy a few good mares and a stallion to start him off. He gives me an investment tip now and then in return. He doesn't run the card game, that kind of thing's too risky and amateur for this bloke. He only sits in on it – in order to make friends. Officially he's in property and development, so he can account for his money if he has to. The cops can't get anything on him, and he's got plenty on them. That's why I was upset when you threatened me in front of him. You've got no idea how careful you gotta be around blokes like that. They're touchy as hell, superstitious and psychological. I don't want to lose his confidence. If I play me cards right, in a year or two, I'll be living in a high-rise on the Gold Coast. You see."

The boys laughed.

Tanner wanted to be impressive.

"That bloke you saw today has a mate who makes weapons in a shed outside Villeneuve. He brings parts from different countries and assembles em out here to avoid being seen. I'm buyin a copy of a sniper rifle from the Balkans war."

"Why the hell would an old bastard like you need a gun like that?' said Eccleston.

Tanner only raised his eyebrows, as though the appeal of owning the weapon was obvious.

Eccleston sighed. He was becoming annoyed. Tanner was talking about things he had not seen, only heard about; and neither of the boys could imagine anything more banal than the underworld Tanner described with envy.

Eccleston tapped Grey on the leg and Grey ignited the engine and shifted the column-shift.

"We're goin if you've got nothin else to talk about, Tanner. All of a sudden I don't want to hear it."

Tanner sneered and twisted his mouth.

"Who just put two hundred bucks in your hand, you ungrateful bastard?'

Eccleston opened and closed his empty hand.

"You'll get it tomorrow." Tanner stood up. "I've had it with your blackfella moods. Like I say, after tomorrow you'll never work for me again."

"Good," said Eccleston.

Tanner walked away and Eccleston sighed. Then he laughed.

"Just imagine the old bastard in a Gold Coast penthouse, watchin bikini girls through binoculars!'

"Or through the scope on his sniper rifle," Grey smiled. "He'll fit in fine."

They both laughed, and Grey took the truck onto the road.

"I'm thirsty," said Eccleston.

"Me too."

They drove to the Railway Hotel. They walked past the old men who sat morning until night on the veranda watching the sky. Grey put twenty dollars on the bar and the boys drank pots of bitter and watched rain fall in sheets on the hills.

WHEN HE CAME home Irene was plucking apple-mint leaves from the plants she grew amidst milk thistle. She tried to be angry with him.

"You smell like a horse," she said.

"I thought you liked the smell."

"You stink," she smiled.

In the kitchen she crushed the mint leaves into tea that was stewing in a pot on the stove. The smell drifted through the room. She put a cup in Grey's hands.

For dinner they ate reheated corned brisket and boiled vegetables. Irene cut wedges of butter and slapped them on her potatoes and cauliflower. Grey told her when she grew up she'd be enormous.

She smiled and stuck a fork into a potato.

"Gotta grease em else they won't go down."

For afters she had a spoon of days' old bread-and-butter pudding. She made Grey promise to take her to the northern hills in the morning, to a little stream where fish gathered at the piles of an old rail bridge. She fell asleep on the floorboards in the breeze that rushed through the open front door.

Grey sat up and read from a leather-bound notebook he had found in a chest that belonged to his mother. He ran his thumb slowly across the handwritten words, across the indents made by the nib of his mother's pen. He listened to the wind in the leaves of the stringybark, then to a Mass by Pärt on the radio.

A horse turned around in the dark outside and he remembered Tanner and the slick-haired criminal at the yards. He wondered how much of what Tanner had said was true.

# VI

IRENE WOKE HIM EARLY THE NEXT MORNING. SHE SAT
on the end of his bed and held his ear until he groaned.

He went down to the truck to rig the handlines. She came
buttoning her shirt and carrying a thermos of last night's tea
and a lunchbox of corned meat and mustard sandwiches along
with a half-dozen cold potatoes she had boiled the night before
and wrapped in foil. It was near seven and already warm and it
would be hot by the time they got to the creek.

They drove onto Wivenhoe-Somerset Road and left the car
in front of Eli's Shoppe at the junction of the two big lakes and
walked into the woods. They walked across a splintering of nameless creeks and gullies. Grey made sure they kept their line by
lining up distinctive trees in the direction they wanted. When he
drew close to one tree he lined up the second with a farther
third. Irene laughed and said she did not need to mark the trees
to find her way, but she followed her brother.

They came out of the woodland into open country where
the water gouged a meadow of wildflowers. They set up near a
long-unused girder: a warped structure of railway sleepers that
had usurped their bolts and given over wholly to the commands
of the weather.

The creek was not six yards across at its widest so they
more dropped their lines in than cast. Black she-oaks and grey
gums hugged the bank and sunlight filtered through the trees
and lit the water that flowed clear and fast over the ribbed bed.

Rocks and overhanging tree roots made shadowy pools where a fish might rest. Grey and Irene sat on the bank and drank tea from their thermos and took cold water up from the stream in their hands.

Irene skittered her hook over the water. Grey did not watch his line. He watched the tops of the she-oaks being smudged by the thumb of the wind, the clear water polishing stones.

At eight o'clock they sat barefoot in the shade of a gigantic grey gum. They ate their sandwiches and listened to the water. Irene would be an hour late for school, but her teacher was accustomed to that.

"Why does food always taste better outside?' she asked.

"You earn it walking, I spose."

She looked in the canvas bag at the one big eel-tailed catfish they had caught.

"You can eat catfish," Irene declared.

She had eaten it often enough in years gone by, when Grey did not have the two hundred dollars a week he made at the service station now.

"This boy is old, though. There'd be more silt in him than on the bottom of this creek. We'll put him in Ook's bathtub to drain him out. He'll be right to eat in time."

Irene nodded.

"How come you don't take Vanessa fishing?"

"I don't know."

"She's too dainty," said Irene. "And she's probably afraid of fish slime."

"Probably."

She took the catfish up out of the bag and kissed its lips and whiskers and then grimaced. "You poor old man."

Grey smiled.

"Will you come get me after school," she said, "so we can muck around tonight?"

"I'm working at the service station."

"I don't mind the service station."

"If you like."

"It'll mean I won't have to wait all night at the restaurant with old Minh rousing on me."

"Then I'll pick you up."

She was pleased.

"I'm different to Vanessa, Grey."

He smiled at the childish competition for his attention. But then a look came to her face that was not childish, one of deep, abstracted thought.

He did not ever truly know what she was thinking.

"What do you mean?' he asked.

She did not answer him. She curled her toes in the fine gravel at the edge of the water.

He wondered at the strange moods that seemed to visit her from without. He remembered the night their grandmother died: Irene had had delirious dreams that she could not be woken from. She had sat up suddenly. According to their father it was the minute that Margaret Finnain died.

"Grey."

"Yes?"

She turned away from him and threw the crust of her sandwich in the creek. She watched the lambent light on the water, stared intently into that other world into which Grey could not see but by the impression it made upon her.

"You'll keep me now – you won't leave me?"

Grey furrowed his brow. Twice lately she had spoken words akin to this. He wondered why. Perhaps she thought of their father, who had left them for so long when she was younger.

"I've taken care of you this long. I'm not about to stop."

She sighed.

"You treat me different to Vanessa. Is it because you don't think I'm pretty? Is it because I'm your sister?"

"You are pretty."

"You don't believe it. I know when you're lying, Grey." She

stood up and brushed the earth and leaves from her skirt and shins. "Come on, let's go."

It was too hot to fish anymore. They made their way back through the wood.

They stopped to rest on a buttressing quandong root. Irene had carried with her the last exchanges of the conversation on the creek.

"It doesn't matter anyhow. I own you. All things belong to the people who love them most."

SHE DID NOT go to school. She waited at the gate until her brother's truck was out of sight. She walked across the disused railway tracks, stopping to scratch the nose of a long-haired highland pony that lent over rusted barbed wire. She walked past the sweet-smelling sawmill to climb her favourite fig tree. She stayed cradled in a massive bough, daydreaming, half-sleeping through the afternoon until Eccleston's truck pulled up beside her.

"How long's school been taught in trees?"

She shrugged and smiled.

"Where are you going?"

"Into the hills to check traps. You want to come?"

He had meant this as a joke. Girls were uncomfortable around him at the best of times, without the sanguinary facts of the way he made his living. He had an intimidating frame, and he was half-caste. He knew parents told their children even worse stories about half-castes than full-bloods.

But Irene smiled and climbed down.

He put out his cigarette and cleared the seat for her.

# VII

GREY DROVE TO BIZZELL'S SERVICE STATION AT THE southern edge of town. The owner, Frank Bizzell, was a hermetic and nervous man of sixty odd years who was frightened of missing anyone's money as they rolled through Mary Smokes. On a whim he would ask Grey to keep the service station open until midnight rather than close at a sensible hour. Then Grey was meant to sleep in a fold-out iron bed in the back room, to guard the money. Bizzell did not trust him to take the cashbox home.

There were three old latch-handle pumps out front braced by transplanted palms. The palms and a shabby wooden toilet and one yellow-flowering wattle tree were festooned with Christmas lights regardless of the season. Bizzell lived in Ipswich now and after a certain hopeless hour there was no one to stop Grey doing as he pleased. When it was quiet he would sit and read newspapers from the rack.

He read again of the man who had been killed on Highway 54. The newspaper said the "violent event" was still unresolved and likely ever would be. He thought how someone could drive a man off the road here in the middle of the night and be at the far north coast or the desert the next day. He put the paper down and looked toward the invisible highway. He wondered why the man in the newspaper story was killed. Drugs. A gambling debt. Perhaps he was a police informer. And perhaps he was killed for nothing – idiocy and boredom. You could not know. You could not assume anything had a meaning anymore. And those perhaps-murderers had fled into oblivion and impunity on the highway that even now might be concealing them at unmemorable stops, amidst people in transit who did not recognize that anyone belonged to any place, and so could not tell fugitives apart.

He was near asleep in his chair when Angela came in to the counter. He checked the clock on the wall that showed three empty revolutions must be made before midnight. Angela's hair was out of the careful place she always set it. Her eyes were bloodshot and weepy with tiredness.

"I thought you were at the restaurant," Grey said.

"No. It's just old Minh and his wife tonight. I've been to Toogoolawah, to the bridge club."

No money ever changed hands and no serious cards were played at the house party called the bridge club. Instead it gave occasion for a number of the district's bored wives to get distract-edly drunk.

Angela put an orange juice on the counter.

"Also a packet of menthols."

Then Grey remembered Irene. He had forgotten to collect her from school. No doubt she had waited.

He took the cigarettes from the stand behind him. Angela handed him a ten-dollar note and leant on her elbows on the counter.

"Are you all right?' He put her change down in front of her.

She stayed leaning on the counter, now with her head on her forearms. She was drunker than even her eyes had told.

"How did you get home?"

"The bus. I took the bus."

There was a late-night bus that passed through Toogoola-wah, but Grey was sure it made its last trip an hour ago. The road from there to here was completely unlit. She must have walked, else fallen asleep at the Mary Smokes bus shelter and only now woken up.

"Sit down for a bit."

He took a chair from the back room and set it down beside her.

"How are your bridge friends?"

"Tolerable. Barely."

He could imagine. He had met a few of them.

Angela picked up a women's magazine and began leafing through it. She stopped at a picture of a European prince having his boots shined on a cluttered street, perhaps in the Americas, while his heavily made-up princess looked on smiling.

Angela sighed. "I'd polish boots forever if just for one day someone would polish mine. Just once to feel important."

Grey could think of no response to such a strange remark.

She collected her cigarettes and juice from the counter and stood up.

"I'm all messed up tonight, Grey. Don't take any notice of me."

"Why don't you rest here a while?"

"Can I smoke?"

"Sure."

She sat down again and lit a cigarette.

"Thank you. You're very kind. I've told you that before. You have a kind face, you know?"

He forced a smile. Angela dragged heavily on her cigarette.

"Can I say something serious to you?"

"Of course."

"I'm not well suited to family life, Grey. That's why I chose badly the first time around – a husband, I mean. I didn't choose a proper man but a criminal. You know, he couldn't sleep in the moonlight," she laughed. "He was crazy. He'd sit alone at the saleyards where he worked, all night long in a two-metre square dogbox and watch the empty road and drink. I couldn't have chosen worse. It sort of ruined me for everything that came after. I hope you understand." She sighed. "Do you have an ashtray? And I was pretty enough when I was younger. Plenty of men would've had me." She stared out the window. "I'm not much of a mother to Irene. I don't need to tell you that. Anyway, she has no time for me. That's natural."

"She likes you."

"Oh yes, very mildly. I'm not a good mother, Grey. I'm not a companion to your father, either. You know that too. Though I try, with my limited abilities. I was pretty once," she repeated sadly. "Once I could've had anyone. You want to know something ridiculous? I thought since at least one beautiful girl had loved your father, well – that he would look after me."

Grey did not say that marital happiness was as foreign to their house in the time of his mother as it was now, more so; so foreign that neither he nor Irene knew what gestures it made, only that it was absent.

He wished he had remembered Irene tonight. He wondered what she was doing. Probably mopping out the kitchen of the restaurant, tired by now with the work and with trying to understand Minh Quy's broken English.

All at once Angela became embarrassed by what she had said. They fell into a long unbroken silence. Grey looked out the window and lapsed into a desultory gaze over the outskirts of town. The grass and sorghum, the iron pylons ...

"I can take you home if you like."

"What time do you finish here?"

"Not till twelve, but I can shut the place up and drive you."

"No. Thanks. I'll walk."

"It won't take two minutes to close up."

"Could you?"

On the drive he thought about going to get Irene, but guessed she was asleep at Amy's.

WHEN GREY RETURNED, the service station was enveloped by silence. The clock lost its power to describe time, and the shapeless hours of time out of time were coming. Those hours came falling in the dark outside to isolate the roadhouse from the world of sleeping men and women awaiting tomorrow.

He sat on a step of concrete at the back of the service station and looked up at the Milky Way. Sirius burned brightly in the northeast. He could not name the other stars without Irene. There was no point watching the road. Nobody else was stopping. He lay against the wall beside the back door to observe the vigilance that at this hour became absurd. There was no one coming and no one to watch him waiting for no one to come and so no reason to stay.

He did not know he had fallen asleep when her voice perforated his dreams.

"You forgot me."

"I'm sorry. You should have asked Minh to take you home."

He rubbed his eyes and looked inside at the clock. The restaurant would have closed long ago. He knew now she had gone to Amy's house and stayed up with her in order to make him worry. And he had fallen asleep.

"Let's go. I can get up early and come back. I wonder should I leave the truck here, in case old Bizzell comes by in the morning. I can get Ook to drop me back."

"Leave it here. I feel like walking."

So he left the floodlight on and left his truck parked out front as it should be and they walked home in the dark.

IRENE TIED HER hair and walked barefoot on the asphalt. She carried the new shoes Grey had bought her that had given her blisters. He took a squashed packet of cigarettes from his jeans and lit one. No cars passed them. At the bottom of Solitary Hill they looked up and saw the giant white drive-in screen. Then came the plain and glistening crops. Then they were home.

ANGELA WAS DRUNK and asleep and their father was at the railway. Grey and Irene lounged in the living room in a breeze that ebbed and flowed through the house. The walk home had more excited them than made them sleepy. It was half-past two. Irene lit a kerosene lamp. The house had electric light – and electricity when Grey or Angela remembered to pay the bill – but the girl had grown up with firelight.

He knew he should send her to bed as tomorrow was another school day. But they talked of their mother. As always he was disappointed at how little he remembered. He wanted to tell his sister stories from his own experience, but most of what he had, that formed any kind of narrative, were second-hand accounts. And his own few stories she had heard many times. He had used them up. He possessed fragments now, flashes of isolated detail.

He told her that their mother could speak Irish.

"She spoke it to me sometimes." *Ish misha* Grey, he remembered. That was all.

He stood up and went to a red-painted tin chest in the room where Angela lay insensible between a bottle of bourbon and the same magazine full of aristocrats, film stars and business people she had flicked through at the service station. He returned to the living room and handed his sister a leather-bound quarto.

"Here," he said.

"What is it?"

"It's our mother's. Grandma said this is her writing – a few poems and notes, but mostly lessons in Irish."

Irene's dark eyes ran across her mother's handwriting. The writing was made at the same age she was now. She palmed a photograph that fell out of its place in the pages and onto the floor. The photograph was the same Grey always kept, that he had used as a bookmark since he began perusing the notebook without comprehension a fortnight ago.

"Do you think I follow her?"

"Grandma saw a resemblance."

Irene ran her fingers around the rusty edge of the photograph then placed it back in the notebook.

"You have her smile," Grey said at last. Then he felt he must be dreaming. As she knelt on the floor before him in the

attitude of study, he realized that mother and daughter were all
but identical. She shifted her feet beside her, raised her face
and furrowed her brow to ask what he was looking at. The vision
did not vanish.

How had he not seen it before? Were he asked to describe
their common features he would have been at a loss; besides
the polarity of their hair colour, their mother's eyes were blue
where Irene's were darkest brown; and where their mother's
skin was golden and perfect, Irene's was pale and her cheeks
were wind-burnt red. Yet for all that, he saw now there were
certain habitual gestures – the eyes-closed smile, the furrowed-
brow frown – gestures that recalled his mother perfectly.

She was attempting to pronounce the letters her mother
had written as though they were Australian English letters.
Then she affected an Irish accent. Grey was sorry that there was
no one to teach her. He might have learnt once, but he had
been lazy; when his mother had spoken to him in that language
he had pretended not to hear her. Now he wished he had not
been lazy. He imagined what it would be to speak with her in a
language no one else, not Angela, not the town, not even their
father, would understand. Such could never be a dead language.
Irene looked up at him and made her mother's frown.

"You're laughing at me."

"No."


SHE WENT FOR a bath before bed and Grey sat on the rise
behind the house. He had not slept and there was no point going
to sleep now. He would walk soon to get Eccleston to drive him.
The wind came through the leaves of the stringybark and lemon
tree. He looked away, but then looked back through the glass
where the orange bathroom lamp lit his sister. With her back to
him she took off her dress. There was nothing without the
window but sorghum fields and grassland and so no reason for
shame and she never drew the blind. She coughed and let go
the tie in her hair. He watched her undress and run the shower.

Her body glowed in the lamplight. Her body that had so long resisted time – as though informed by her innocent spirit – tonight was not quite the body of a little girl. She coughed again into her hands. Was she getting a cold, even in summer? With the thought an unaccountable tenderness came over him. He had allowed her to stay up too late. She stepped into the water.

He laughed at himself. He watched the night until the lights of the flats and hills gave no more perspective and he was sitting in a box of floating ornaments, earth and sky and he, all floating as in the fancy of a childish mind. Then came the dawn.

# VIII

GREY SLEPT LATE INTO THE MARCH AFTERNOON THEN
set out for the big highway and the Helidon freight yards for a
night's work.

After two hours loading and unloading seed, poison and a
few cars of cattle and horses, he pencilled KL142, the last car
of the penultimate train of the night, into the logbook and took
it to his father who was talking with the train driver.

"There you go, old man."

"Did you get em all right?"

"Yep."

Grey sat down on the bonnet of his truck and watched
thirty-three cars of freight squall into the east. It was half-past
eight. The night had become cool with the promise of rain.
Bill North came to sit beside Grey and though he was silent, Grey
could tell the prematurely old man had something to say. He
rolled a cigarette with nervous hands, and his pale-blue eyes,
that always seemed to betray some deep inner weakness,
skittered about the night. He picked at the stained calluses on
his hands.

"You know, boy, I've been thinkin you might be better off
goin to work in the city, or somewhere else other than Mary
Smokes. Gettin yourself a proper job."

Grey nodded.

"You're young. I reckon you must know what kinds of jobs
are out there for young men. Somethin you don't have to work

too hard at. Somethin where you're somebody ... So you don't end up like your old bloke."

A part of Bill North's heart had been missing or was twisted and he had been incapable of loving his children as a father. But he had come to respect Grey as a man. And the man's sincerity moved the son. It upset Grey to hear his father confess to him like this, but he could not object. To have told the man he was doing all right in the world would have been such an obvious lie as to make the shame of it greater. All Bill North's hopes for the future now lay in a change to the government's pension laws and a doubtful claim that had not come through in six months since it was lodged.

"You must have thought of it," Bill North said. "Of gettin out."

"I have, old man. I spose I have."

"Seriously? You've thought seriously about it then?"

"Yes," Grey lied.

"I'm glad to hear it. You don't have to tell me what you're thinkin. Work it out for yourself, then just get up and go. Nothin'd make me happier."

"All right."

"There's no future in a town like this anymore, boy. You stay here, you don't make somethin of yourself now, and people less than you will be treadin on you all your life."

"I know it."

"You've got to think about providin for a woman one day too. There's always that. Women don't want to be poor."

The night before Angela last left for her sister's, she and his father had fought. It was late and they were shut in their room, but Grey could hear plainly through the walls their fighting over things that marked the narrow limits of their affection.

"I did go to the doctor," Bill North had said with as much force as unvoiced speech can have. "He's ordered pills that will work better."

"And your drinking all night, do you think that'll help?' she said with perfect hypocrisy. "You know, I don't feel like a woman anymore!"

Grey knew the things they fought over did not become serious if there was enough money and material comfort to atone for them. That night he had gone into Irene's room and found her lying awake in the dark. He sat down on the end of her bed and told stories to keep her from the argument. Eventually he fell asleep beside her.

"You're a bright boy," Bill North said. "Even the blokes here at the railways give you a natural respect they never give me. I don't pretend to talk to you as a clever man, but I've seen things. I'd talk to Irene too, only she's young. That poor girl." Grey watched his father's hands tremble. At any other time he would have put the trembling down to want of drink. Bill North clenched his fists to make the trembling stop. "Damn it, I should do better."

Grey stood up and put his hand on his father's shoulder to end the talk.

"Don't worry about me, old man. I'm workin somethin out." He lied again for the sake of peace.

WORK AT THE freight yard meant driving through Haigslea, past Vanessa's. Most nights nothing came of that, he would finish too late. Tonight he called her from a public phone box on the roadside and told her he might be around.

"Last train is late, boy," said his father when he got back. "You go if you like."

Grey was happy. He was bodily tired, fifty dollars up and free of obligation. He was not concerned about leaving his father now. The train to come was just a handful of cars.

HE STOPPED BY the Sundowner bottle shop on the way. He hid his truck on a dirt road behind Vanessa's house.

"I didn't expect you for another hour."

"I got off early. Here."

He handed her a bottle of ten-dollar sparkling white wine. She put the bottle in ice on the coffee table. She took two crystal glasses from a cabinet.

Vanessa's house seemed very fancy to Grey. Leather lounge chairs, polished teak cabinets and carpeted floors.

"Come sit down," she said.

She folded her legs beside her on the lounge, revealing much of her tanned thighs. She wore her white frilled cardigan, and a gold crucifix hung around her neck. Her church clothes. When she was home Vanessa was a regular at the Friday night service at the highway's boxcar Presbyterian Church. There the travelling minister spoke his excited sermons after the manner he had seen on television to a gathering that was outnumbered three to one by the crowd across the asphalt at the hotel. Vanessa smelled of church. Grey had not been in years but he remembered the smell. He wondered was it beeswax candles, or the starched clothing of the elderly, or the varnish on the pews.

"Irene's got one of these," he said, touching the crucifix where it rested on Vanessa's bare skin. "A nun gave it to her. Hers is Benedictine."

Vanessa smiled doubtfully. She did not know what Benedictine meant. In that country, expressions of orthodox faith were almost non-existent. Those who did not remember Grey's mother and the old Irish and Russians of the district thought Irene's religiosity uniquely childish and fantastical.

"This?' she caught his hand. "It protects me."

"From what?"

"Those who would cause the innocent to sin."

He smiled.

"You know, I admire you – going to church when your folks aren't here to force you."

"They have spies. If I hadn't gone tonight they would have heard about it. Anyway, you don't admire it. Everyone who says that says it condescendingly."

"You're wrong."

She smiled provocatively. "How come you never go? You're Catholic, aren't you?"

"I have belief. My God is present late at night, in silence, in running water, with people in pain."

Vanessa looked at him with bemusement.

"Churches these days are different. The one I go to in the city draws four or five hundred to every service, most of them under forty, and there's even a stage for a band, and a café. It's fun. You should come one day."

Grey sighed.

"Don't you sometimes think we're meant to suffer – that we've brought it on ourselves? The sin is in us and it's just a trick of time that means we must wait to commit it."

"How awful!"

"Yes," he said.

He lent across her body and took the wine from the table. "Drink?"

"Sure." She picked up a glass. "Tell me something, Grey."

For a moment he thought this was going to be something serious. He did not feel like speaking seriously tonight.

"How did Flagon Norman get his name?"

Grey smiled and took his knife from his jeans and unfastened the file and levered the cork. He filled Vanessa's glass.

"On the night of our school graduation he stole a flagon of goon wine and disappeared into the woods. The police found him the next day asleep on the creek. And his mother had dressed him up so nice in his father's old tartan coat and green tie. I spose he got scared. He wasn't used to so many people. Once he left the hall he would have just walked till he fell. He's got bad eyes. He's near blind at night. But he hung onto the flagon. He was nursing it when they found him."

Vanessa could not stop giggling.

Then Grey told her the story of when Raughrie Norman drove his first and only car into the ground:

"No one told him you had to put oil in it. He was between

Mary Smokes and Toogoolawah when the bearings blew and it seized up. He just got out and left it on the road and walked."

So the night flowed away, with talk of inane local things and of ill-defined future plans of escape that Grey did not believe. Worn out with the night's work and pacified by the wine, he fell asleep in Vanessa's arms before anything they had wordlessly planned had happened. The call of a freight train woke him. It was after eleven.

Vanessa's parents were at a government function in the city and they would not always pay for a motel. They might be back any minute now depending on how late the thing ran.

"I spose I'd better go."

"I guess so," Vanessa said, rousing herself from sleep.

"You know, you can come home with me if you like."

"How?"

"Tee it up with a friend. Give someone a call and get them to cover for you. You can say you stayed at their place after church. Say you felt lonely."

"I couldn't. I've only got one girlfriend here and it's too late to call her now."

"It'd be good if you could."

"Really, I couldn't."

"Well, I should go."

She said goodnight and kissed his lips.

He walked down the stairs onto the road.

THE SOUTH WIND blew a light spray of rain across the plain and the asphalt glistened in the moonlight. Grey's eyes wandered up to the highway, to a billboard he had not seen before, that announced a recently arrived church. He wondered if it was a branch of the church Vanessa had spoken of. The church's billboard presented a prosperous-looking travesty of Christ: his hair as well-kept as a banker's, and the wounds of the Cross like neat red medallions in his hands.

On the street her voice came after him and then the fast shuffle of her feet.

"Grey! Maybe I will come. I guess I will."

He stopped and waited for her to catch up.

"How far away did you park?

He pointed to an empty street.

She giggled, tickled at the trouble he had gone to for her.

ANGELA WAS STILL awake when they arrived at Grey's house. She sat in the living room reading a magazine by lamplight. A bottle of brandy and one of sleeping pills sat on the table beside her.

"Grey, you should tell me when you're bringing friends home. Forgive the state of the house," she said to Vanessa.

"Vanessa, you know Angela."

Vanessa did not say anything. She was still a little drunk from the wine. She had sipped the last of the bottle in Grey's truck.

"Hello, Mrs North."

Grey smiled at Angela and she smiled back. She did not ever call herself Mrs North.

"Bill'll be here shortly," Grey said. "The last train was pulling out when we left Haigslea."

"There's food on the stove if you want it," said Angela. "Leave some for Bill."

Vanessa said it was sweet that Angela waited up for her husband.

Grey smiled.

They moved into the kitchen and he opened the lid on a pot of beef stew.

"Want some?"

Vanessa eyed the contents of the pot with suspicion and shook her head.

He walked down the corridor and opened a crack in Irene's

doorway and saw her swathed in white sheets, lying facing the wall and window, her dark hair spilled across the pillow.

"Is she asleep?' Vanessa whispered.

Grey nodded.

They went to his bedroom and sat down on the bed. He lit the bedside lamp.

"Why don't you have decorations on your walls?' she asked. "It's depressing, Grey. Like your name."

He looked around the room. He had not realized.

"What sort of a name is Grey anyway?"

"It's Greywood. My mother gave it to me. After the woods she used to walk on Mary Smokes Creek."

"I'm sorry." Vanessa wondered if she had offended him. "I was only joking."

She kissed him. He did not feel what a man was supposed to feel. Perhaps it was the wine. She shifted closer and he moved his hands under her blouse and she pushed him down on the bed. He turned off the light. In the dark she stretched out across his body and kissed him again and a pain came to the small of his back.

In time all the lights in the house were off. Grey heard his father come home and after that there was quiet. The blue light of the moon came in through the window. Outside, the wind rose and the branches of the stringybark bent to touch the house. The branches were like rain on the corrugated-iron roof.

VANESSA WAS ASLEEP. Grey got out of bed and opened the door to see what the crying was. She was crouched in the dark beside his door. Her head was against her knees that were in her arms. Moonlight arced across the hall from the living room and lit her tiny feet.

"What's the matter?"

He whispered so as not to wake the house. He knelt on the floor beside her. He put his hand on her cheek that was wet with crying and pushed a tear-soaked lock of hair behind her ear.

She brushed his hand away and stood up. She ran out the door and across the yard in her nightdress.

Eccleston's grass moved in long fluid waves and she stood at the edge of it. When she saw that he followed she crawled through the wire. She ran further away. He called into the wind. He pulled the wires apart and stepped through.

He ran after her and caught her shoulder.

She had cut her hand on the barbs and he saw the blood on her nightdress. She took his hand and put it to her wet cheek. The sight of her blood brought tears to his eyes. His own blood surged through his body and he shivered though the night was not cold.

"We have to go back to the house."

"Why?' She turned away from him. She faced the western plain.

"Because we can't stay here all night."

"I can."

"Look there." And he pointed to the south where a green-flickering storm had shut out the stars. "These are games for children, Irene."

She shook her head.

He held her shoulders. She stood on her toes and reached up toward him but he caught her face in his hands and squeezed her jaw as though he were a beast trapping prey. He stared at her with eyes she had never seen. She shuddered. She cried and pulled out of his grip. She stood trembling before him and he must do something to reassure her.

"It's just that you're a little girl, Irene. I'm nothing big like you think."

The awful look on his face was gone, and his words made her smile through her tears. She choked and laughed.

"When did I say you were anything big? I know who you are, little boy."

She had spoken from out of an almost forgotten dream, sounded an echo that time had almost obliterated, that now obliterated time. He held her shoulders again. Again she was frightened. Again he stared into her deep sad eyes. He felt her trembling.

"Don't send me mad, Irene. I won't be mad."

He let her go and turned his back on her and walked back across the grass. She stood still and watched him go and put her face in her hands.

He turned again at the fenceline. The wind tore at his words.

"I'm going home," he said. "You follow me."

Vanessa woke when he came in, but soon returned to sleep, and in her dreams his strange movements were forgotten. He watched Eccleston's from the window of his room. He did not see her come in, but guessed she soon would. Outside the wind kept up and then came the storm. Inside the house the storm was all he could hear.

# IX

SHE MIGHT HAVE SAT UP ON THE STAIRS, OR GONE TO sleep in a chair on the veranda. The storm had lasted until dawn and he could not have heard the absence of her steps on the floorboards. He told himself he could not have known she did not return.

He drove Vanessa to Highway 54 and put her on the bus and went looking for his sister. When she was not at Amy's, nor the bend in the creek, nor the lake, nor anywhere within calling distance of them, he began to fear for her. The storm had grown fierce through the night. She was only a child, but she was solemn and resolute. She might have struck off anywhere. And in such a storm, in the dark, she might have been blinded and fallen. He looked across the calm water of the lake that belied the night gone.

He told his father and then called the police. Bill North, the local sergeant, a constable from Toogoolawah and the Mary Smokes boys set about finding her.

By midday a dozen townspeople were added to the party, persuaded by the sergeant. Most said the girl was a fool and was likely only hiding. But by late afternoon there was still no sign of her.

It became dark and the official search was called off until morning. A car would patrol the Valley Highway through the night.

The sergeant stood with Grey on the road outside the plywood station and rolled a cigarette.

"Does she know anyone in the near towns? In the city?"

Grey said she did not. He had to tell the sergeant she was in the habit of walking off, even at night. The townswomen would only say the same. The sergeant nodded and lit his cigarette and the valley wind sent ash and sparks flying from its end into the dark.

"She's probably been caught in the rain. Stayed in some abandoned hut in the hills."

But Grey knew she could find her way back from anywhere in this country in a day.

Later even the townswomen became concerned. At the town hall a group of them who would normally not have seen Grey or his father fit to speak to offered them supper.

"We've got to keep looking," Grey said to Eccleston over a plate of thin stew. Eccleston nodded.

THE BOYS RE-CHECKED the road that went into the D'Aguilar Range. They stopped Grey's truck at every creek and gully that ran beneath or beside the road and walked along it in pairs up and down stream. They walked to the sources of streams then came back to the road. If she was lost she knew to keep to the creeks, though it seemed impossible that she could ever be lost in the woods of the valley or the mountains.

The sky began to pale in the east and a cool westerly scattered the clouds in a single dry breath. The stormy summer night that initiated this trouble seemed a thousand miles away. The cool became cold and still they did not find her. They made it to the cedar flats before the climb into the mountains proper. They stopped the truck midway between Red and White Cedar creeks. Raughrie Norman and Thiebaud walked along White Cedar, and Grey and Eccleston along Red Cedar. The trees were thick along the banks and Eccleston and Grey walked through running water in the bed.

Raughrie Norman called out to them though they could not make out the words. They ran back to the road. They ran to where the boy had set off along White Cedar Creek and saw him ducking in and out of trees, coming toward them with Irene cradled in his arms, her own pale arms dangling at her sides like a doll's.

He said he had found her in the creek. She had been caught and tripped in wire. He presented her to Grey and whimpered like a child at her state. Grey's relief at finding his sister disappeared. Her clothes were wet and filthy. Her feet were cut to shreds. Barbed wire was wrapped tight around her ankles. The skin was red and hot where the wire bit it. Grey ran his fingers over the deepest wounds that were leaking. Her forehead was like a stove iron. Her breath was shallow. She babbled and then said she was hot and wanted to drink.

Grey wrapped her in his oilskin coat and set her down on the passenger seat of the truck. He cut away the wire with pliers and eased the barbs from her skin.

"I waited for you, but you didn't come," she said. "I was looking for home, but I couldn't find it."

"She's delirious," Grey said to Eccleston. To her, "Just rest and don't talk."

Grey held her up and helped her drink from his canteen. With Irene lying down there was no more room in the truck. The boys walked down the road toward town. Having come so far Grey knew he must drive on to Brisbane and to the first hospital he found. He pulled the truck hard around the mountain turns and arrived at the Emergency door at a west-side hospital called the Wesley. He explained to a young triage nurse what had happened and she wrote it down. The nurse told Grey that this was a private hospital. He said it did not matter. She asked for a name and an address,

"One of the girl's parents. Or a guardian."

"Grey North," he said.

But when he could not tell the nurse what allergies the girl had, she raised her eyebrows.

The doctor said Irene had blood poisoning, made worse by two nights' exposure. The nurses attached her to an oxygen machine. Grey's eyes met his sister's through the window of the private room where she lay. She was so sick she seemed not to recognize him. She turned away. A nurse put a cannula in her arm to inject fluid and antibiotics and she did not wince, nor did she when the doctor drained the abscesses and cleaned the wounds on her feet and ankles with tweezers and a scalpel. Grey heard the doctor tell a nurse that the deep splinters must come out with the pus. The nurse wrapped Irene's feet with gauze. Grey went in and held his sister's hand and she did not open her eyes.

NURSES FINISHED THEIR shifts and new nurses began and no one at the hospital seemed to recognize his association with the little girl in the room anymore. No one had spoken to him since the brief few words when he admitted her.

Her pathetic little body lay in the room where he sometimes stood at the window and watched the nurses replace the drip and review the machine that monitored her blood pressure. He had never seen a human being so physically incapable of suffering as Irene must have suffered in two wet and cold nights alone in the woods.

He sat in the ward's waiting room and stared at a picture. A seascape rendered in pastels. He walked back to Irene. She was lying on her back and her eyes were closed. He stood in the corridor.

When one of the attending nurses walked by, Grey grabbed her arm. He apologized.

"Is she all right?"

"Who?"

"Irene North. The girl in that room."

The nurse looked back over her shoulder.

The nurse must have been conscious of him sitting in the hallway and the lounge and only now knew his purpose.

"You're a relative?"

"I'm her brother."

"And her parents?"

He shook his head.

"She was in shock, but not now."

GREY HELD HIS sister's hand and now and then her dark eyes opened and spoke to him.

In time she took off her oxygen mask and complained about her bed covers being too hot. Grey kissed her soft, flushed cheek. He would have taken her up in his arms but for the apparatus still attached to her and the fear of doing her harm. Instead he slid his chair even closer and put his shoulder against hers and held her hand while she slept.

DUSK GATHERED WITHOUT the window and the city showed him the same sparkling and tranquil and lonely face as those years ago when Irene was born. He stayed with her until ten.

He took a meal of fish and chips at the hospital cafeteria. The only hotels he knew were north of the city near the airport. He left his truck in the hospital car park that had closed for the night and took a train to the north and walked Kingsford Smith Drive until he found a cheap room. He spent a quarter of his money on a simple, clean room for three nights at a motel called the Hacienda.

WHEN HE WAS not at the hospital he walked aimlessly around the northwestern suburbs. He took meals at one or another of the fish and chip shops or kebab joints between fancier eateries, and felt a quiet, slow-burning peace. He was anonymous, and walked the city like a ghost. He had no worldly thing pressing on him. He had a visit to his sister to look forward to, either that evening or the following day, and the comfort of knowing she was cared for.

At his sister's bedside they did not talk about what had happened. He wondered at her resolve that night. He wondered how many girls would have the courage to walk through a storm in the dark, to satisfy any obstinacy, through even a little pain... Perhaps their existence in Mary Smokes was ridiculous, untenable. He felt so here in the city, amidst so much material progress and so many people. He felt like a relic of a country that existed only in the dreams of a few old men and lost boys. One day there will be no Mary Smokes, he thought. There will only be the city. Mary Smokes will be a name. Then not even a name.

He looked across her bed, through a window to the twinkling streets.

"Don't you want more than our life in Mary Smokes, Irene? To be something in the world?"

"I'd be happy to be no one, but you be something if you want."

How easily she could defeat him.

He had dinner with her that night in the hospital café. She ate potato and leek soup and chocolate cake. After dinner he was sorry to leave her, but the nurses insisted on observance of visiting hours.

Grey left the hospital and walked to the Regatta Hotel at Auchenflower and emptied his wallet on the table and let a waiter take from it and serve him pots of the local bitter. He watched ferries and pleasure boats with festoons of varicoloured bulbs describing their ways along the Brisbane River. No one spoke to him at the hotel and he did not mind. He took the train from Milton to Clayfield and walked across the street from the station to the motel. He could sleep tonight without any trouble in the world to lie down with him. He tried to stay awake to enjoy the feeling. The squalling of city trains stopped at eleven. After that only the occasional freight rushed by. Then the dim drone of trucks on the distant Gateway Motorway. He slept, hardly stirring until morning.

# X

HE LIT A CIGARETTE AND LOOKED OUT THE WINDOW AT
the haying grass rippled by a sunlit March wind, where Irene
and plump little Amy Minh were wading. But for their playful cries
and the wind the land was silent.

His father came in from the railway. Grey watched the
man's work-worn hands tremble as he put his oilskin jacket and
hat on one of a row of black sleeper bolts in a crossbeam. He
watched his daughter and Amy over Grey's shoulder. Irene grimaced and stumbled a little, as she did whenever she stepped too
heavily on the wounded instep of her left foot.

Grey saw Bill North lower his head. Then the man looked
back at Irene.

"Damn it. I should do better," he said.

Grey went to take his father's hand, but the gesture embarrassed the man and he walked off to his liquor cabinet. He
poured himself a Scotch and took the bottle and glass and went
to his room and closed the door.

That night, after a shift at the service station, Grey sat in
the same chair looking out the window and listening to the
radio when Bill North fell in through the door and onto the dining
room table and put his head in his hands. The big man's face
was wet and white with torment.

"Grey, we're in trouble. God, we're in terrible trouble."

Grey looked over his shoulder and down the corridor.

"Irene's asleep," he said. Her door was shut and her light was off. "What the hell's happened?"

Bill North whimpered the story:

"It was her damn hospital bill, Grey. That's what started it. You checked her into a private hospital."

"It was the first on the road."

"Did you see the bill?"

He shook his head. He did not know the bill had come.

"It worked out to three grand."

Grey had not been inside a hospital for fifteen years until that night. He imagined that in an emergency, for those without the means to pay, bed and treatment must cost nothing. His wildest speculation would not have reached three thousand dollars.

"I couldn't pay, Grey. I knew you couldn't either. I went to Tanner."

"Damn it, old man. Surely the hospital would let you pay the money back in stages? Better to owe them money than Tanner."

Bill North had stopped crying now.

Grey breathed deeply.

"So you owe Tanner three grand?"

"I don't owe him anything. He wouldn't lend it. He introduced me at a card game at Dinmore."

Grey was silent. His father looked up.

"I won, Grey. I won big. I quit as soon as I got the sum of the bill. I sent the check the next day. But I went back tonight. I reckoned my luck was in. They suckered me. I tell you, it was for her. I know I've been nothin to you two. If only your mother'd lived and it was me who died, your lives would've been different. She was clever and decent. She could've reared you both properly, not left you on your own. But just once I wanted to do somethin to lift you up a little out of the state I've let you fall to. I'm a weak and stupid man, Grey. I know you believe it. You're right to. But just once I thought I might ..." He raised his head and his bloodshot eyes stared through the wall. "It was for her, Grey. She's

a livin accusation. All I wanted to do was see things righted someway, and then before I knew it I'd bet more than I had. Then
much more. And those men in there … the one who runs the
table … he runs vice in the city. I don't know what he's capable of.
I'd shoot myself here and now if it wouldn't leave us in a worse
mess. I swear to God, I'd do it."

"How much do you owe?"

"Six thousand." The man met his son's gaze. Then he put his
head in his hands again. "Near seven."

Grey closed his eyes.

"Do they know you haven't got it?"

"I couldn't tell em that."

"When are you meant to pay?"

"I've got three weeks. It's gotta be cash. But, Grey. He knows
I have a daughter. He runs all kinds of vice in the city – a brothel
on the outskirts full of underage Filipinos. I've heard it! If a man'll
do that … And what about that bloke who got killed on the
highway in January … The police never caught anyone … I heard
rumours. I'm tired, Grey. So bloody tired."

His father was confused and ranting. Grey thought it
could not be as bad as what he said. But when he walked down
the corridor and looked in on his sleeping sister he felt his
stomach pull tight.

He came back to the living room and picked his father up
by the shirt collar and threw him against the wall. He believed
he would hit him. But he felt pain at his father reduced to nothing
in his hands. He could not hit him or even look him in the eye.

"Go to bed," he said.

He took a half-bottle of Scotch from the table and handed
it to the man and told him again.

Before Grey left the house he returned to his sleeping
sister and kissed her cheek. He thought how awfully simple all
this was. And now how difficult.

# XI

GREY AND ECCLESTON SAT UP THROUGH THE NIGHT WITH
an electric lamp and a tin can ashtray between them on Eccleston's kitchen table. Eccleston broke bits of a rotten cabinet and
fed the potbelly stove. A roll of newspaper gave a false flourish
and then the lacquered wood hissed and spat and gave green
flame. They drank black tea poured from a pot on the stove into
tin cups. A moth flew in through a paneless window and lighted
on the lampshade.

"Tanner is about to take delivery of a deck of quarter
horses," said Eccleston. "Four-year-olds. He's bought em out of
his own pocket. He got caught with em when a client backed
out on a deal. He doesn't know I know. I overheard it a week ago
at the hotel in Toogoolawah. The rate was three grand a head.
Pos might get us somethin like half that, no matter how good the
horses are. Blokes who buy horses off the backs of trucks from
blackfellas without papers know they've got to be sold quick. But
Pos knows people we can sell em to. He's done it before."

"I've got five hundred I can put toward the debt. The old
man's got a couple of head of cattle he can sell. We won't need the
full deck."

"No. Four or five horses. Six to be safe."

"Will Tanner peg it on us?"

"A lot of blokes know he has the horses. Worse blokes than
us."

Grey watched the moth teetering on the inner rim of the lampshade.

He did not want to involve Possum. He had not wanted to involve Eccleston. But he did not know what kind of men these were that his father had become indebted to. His father had been drunk and hysterical. But what if they were truly in danger – and by "they' he meant her alone. Then he would have demanded the names of the men and gone and shot them this night if that would stop it.

"Does Pos see well enough to drive at night?"

"Almost." Eccleston smiled. "But he drives all right. Pos can sell the horses. I don't know if we can. You or me'd draw attention askin about buyers. The people Pos knows are out west. And there's a limit to how far the police will go lookin. Especially for an old blackfella who might not have an address and might disappear into the bush for months, and who most blokes couldn't pick from any other blackfella you stood beside him. But like I say, horses are easy enough for Pos to sell. He knows men who'll put em on trucks at a cattle saleyards where trucks pull up right through the night and no one'll ask any questions. A half-dozen horses'll be taken from nowhere to nowhere else. Maybe for twelve hundred dollars a head."

Eccleston looked up.

"Is it enough?"

"It's enough."

"They're broken, and I reckon they'll be well handled. They'll be catchable. They're in the front paddock on the highway. But there's an access road goin into the hills. You know it. Once they're settled they'll camp in the trees near the creek, not far from that road. Tanner keeps the paddock locked up. The gate chain's that heavy and tight it'd be tough to cut even with bolt cutters. We'll have to cut the fenceline. He might not notice a cut fence for a few hours the next mornin. The truck'll have time to get away, before Tanner realises he's missin horses and goes lookin for em. We'll need one other man. Not Flagon."

"No, not Flagon. If we decide, I'll talk to Thiebaud."

"We don't have much to decide, do we?' Eccleston sighed. "Be discreet, Grey. Tanner's a fool, but the men around him may not be. Say nothin to no one."

Grey nodded and sipped the sweet tea.

"What do you think my old man meant when he said this bloke's dangerous?"

"I don't know. From what I've heard these crime blokes can be as temperamental as children. They might make a big show of gettin a debt back, but then, they might do nothin at all, at least for a while." He sighed. "But finally, they'll insist on gettin paid."

Eccleston did not tell Grey what he had learned at Borallon those years ago. That the moonlight state men used delinquent boys, bikies and ex-inmates to do their dirtiest jobs: men who were not smart enough to stay out of prison or find any other way of getting by. These, once let lose, were uncontrollable. And he did not say he knew a boy from Borallon who was hired to "shadow" a man who owed a bookmaker money; to shoot rat-shot on his roof in the middle of the night, to scratch messages into the panels of his car, and follow his son home from school. Grey looked troubled enough, so Eccleston did not mention these things.

"But I don't know what the blokes at Dinmore are capable of," he said in answer to his own thoughts.

"I'd never ask, Ook."

Eccleston smiled. He tapped the base of the lamp that had flickered off and the filament lit again.

"You're all I have, Grey. You and the boys, and Irene."

Grey did not need to say it was the same for him. He only nodded. He sighed deeply. He rolled a cigarette and struck a match and read the dial of his watch by its light. He lit the cigarette and gave it to Eccleston and rolled another for himself.

The lamp became unnecessary. The moth had disappeared without Grey's noticing.

"Don't tell, Irene, Ook."

Eccleston nodded. Grey frowned.

"I'm sorry. I didn't need to say that."

He stood up from the table and said goodnight and stepped out into the morning twilight.

# XII

THEY WAITED FOR THE NEXT NEW MOON. AT ELEVEN A shredded blanket of cloud separated earth from stars. Wind thumped across the plain from the dry west. The boys climbed into an unregistered bodytruck that Possum had borrowed from a cousin in Lockyer. An outdated set of number plates was on the floor of the cabin, ready to be switched with the present ones tomorrow. The boys drank from a silver flask of whisky to keep warm. They drove toward Highway 54 and turned east down a dirt road. They switched off the headlights and cut the engine and rolled a half-mile in the dark. They eased the truck off the road and down the embankment, close to the fence and the paddock where Tanner's horses stood watching them from their camp.

Eccleston took a pair of pliers from the cabin and cut the three lines of barb and two of plainwire. He cut three inches before the hitches on a split-post and he bent the loose lengths back around a steel post, making a clean ten-foot gap in the fenceline. Grey and Thiebaud collected halters and ropes from the back of the truck, and Possum broke two biscuits of sweet-smelling lucerne hay.

The cloud cover held despite the wind. If anyone passed on the road, all the boys could do was fall to the ground and hope the grass and the dark obscured them. Tanner's house was a half-mile south across Mary Smokes Creek. The lights were all out. On a still night the house was within hearing distance.

The boys hoped the wind that shredded the clouds and whistled in the gullies would obscure their sounds.

They stepped toward the horses. There was a break in the cloud and the stars lit twelve blue-tinged chestnut colts and fillies. The boys became nervous at the clear sight of each other and the horses. Then the starlight was gone again.

Grey broke a hay biscuit and gave half to Eccleston.

Eccleston squatted and whispered and clicked his tongue and held the hay out to the wind and one of the horses lifted its head and turned in the direction of the voice and the boys' hearts beat fast when it came and the others followed.

"Each is as good as the other," Eccleston said to the boys.

Grey drew up to a filly. He squatted below the horse's eye level and looked down at his boots and back to the horse and away again and offered the hay with his extended arm. He shuffled closer and then the filly was sniffing and then nibbling at the hay and Grey scratched her nose and forehead. He rose slowly and stroked the mane. He eased the halter over her ears but the filly snorted and threw her head and the halter fell to the ground.

"Easy, girl. Easy, easy, easy," Grey pleaded.

He re-caught the horse and rubbed his thumb in the concave between its eyes to settle it and fitted the halter and began to lead her. The colt Eccleston was handling whinnied into the wind and stamped hard on the ground. It was a small noise but it seemed tremendous tonight. Grey rechecked the direction of the wind. The sound might not carry far into this, he thought.

"Horses might stir in the night for any reason," Eccleston whispered as they came to the fence, reading his thoughts. Grey nodded.

"A fox or stray dog."

"The wind."

The boys led their horses to the truck where Possum had let down the ramp. They had lain thin mattress on the loading ramp and deck to mute the clattering of hooves. The boys and

Possum looked across to Tanner's house, waiting, expecting, dreading the light that might come on there. But there was no light.

Eccleston's and Grey's horses were loaded, and Grey went to help Possum load Thiebaud's horse and got caught behind it and the horse kicked his shoulder. He fell back with a muted gasp of pain and Eccleston came and raised his head from the dirt. The kick took all the wind from Grey's lungs and his mouth opened wide but admitted only a snatch of breath, and the panic of reaching for air and not finding it came into his eyes. Eccleston rubbed Grey's chest and then Grey found his breath and got to his feet. Eccleston loaded and tethered Thiebaud's horse and Grey led a horse Possum had caught. When the horse pulled back on the lead rope and forced him to use his shoulder he winced.

Hoof thuds and snorts came from the paddock and the boys saw a smoky-black thoroughbred colt pacing the fenceline.

Eccleston spat.

"Damn that horse. He's gonna wake up the house."

Grey squinted into the dark. The horse looked sixteen-and-a-half hands high.

"He's not one of these," said Eccleston.

"What'll we do?"

"We'll take him now he's up here. He'll be the last one. I don't want to frig around any longer."

Grey nodded.

Eccleston walked back into the paddock and focused on the black colt. Even at distance and in the dark the boys could all see what a horse he was, despite an overlong and badly hacked mane: not sixteen-and-a-half but seventeen hands high, and with a white blaze and black coat that flashed in the scraps of starlight that were thrown more frequently earthward now.

With a biscuit of lucerne and tongue clicks Eccleston drew the horse to him. The colt was flighty but curious, and the easiest of the horses to bring within reach. Eccleston stroked its forehead and threw the lead rope around its neck in case the horse spooked. Then he fitted the halter. The colt pulled back and whinnied and grumbled but Eccleston dug his heels and whispered gently and held tight to the rope, and the colt quieted. The boys looked across at the house. Still there was no light.

Eccleston led him through the fence and the colt stepped up onto the truck, his long head nodding up and down, flanks and shoulders quivering and glistening in the scant light. Eccleston wrapped the rope around the rail the other horses were tethered to. Possum lifted the ramp and slid the gate shut and pinned it. Eccleston walked around the side of the truck and climbed up on the wheel and scuttled across the deck untying the horses.

"Let em ride loose. They'll settle on the road."

He eyed the black colt.

"Bloody hell, that's a horse," he said under his breath.

Grey put his foot on the cabin stair and reached for the top of the seat and the pain went right through him. He fell into the cabin. With cuttings of wire Thiebaud and Eccleston made bull-wire knots and twisted three of the fence wires up sufficient to keep the other horses from the road.

They piled into the truck and Possum pulled back up onto the asphalt. The engine worked hard with the load of horses and the boys winced at the sound. They all of them looked again in the direction of Tanner's house. They met the Valley Highway and turned back to the north. Car lights flashed in the distance. When he saw the lights Eccleston reached across Possum and turned on their own lights. The car drew close and then passed, the boys and Possum all looking down to see what it contained. But the car kept innocently on, so perhaps it was only some disoriented tourist.

Possum stopped the truck on the road outside Eccleston's and Grey handed Possum three hundred dollars cash for the trip and shook his hand and the boys got out.

Possum would head west from there on dirt roads until Gatton.

"Then get back on the highway," said Eccleston. "Take the highway in the dark and the back roads in the daylight."

Possum nodded. Eccleston spoke a single word of a language none of the others understood and clasped the old black man's hand. Then the boys shook hands and Eccleston and Thiebaud stepped quickly along the way to the white house on stilts and Grey walked in pain across the grass and then along the gravel to his own house.

He supported his elbow and the weight of his left arm in his right hand. He knew he had broken his collarbone, and that he would have to endure the pain for a week before telling a doctor or anyone else in town about it. He took off his clothes and ran a hot shower.

He wondered where Possum was by now. He went to sleep on his feet in the steaming water.

He boiled water for tea on the potbelly stove. The whistling kettle woke Irene. She came into the living room rubbing her eyes.

"Don't turn on the light."

"Where've you been?' She saw his arm in a sling made of an old shirt. "What happened?"

"I got into a fight. You can't tell anyone."

Irene nodded and asked nothing else, though there were tears in her eyes.

She stayed up with Grey and drank tea and then laid a blanket over him in his bed. She pushed his hair from his face and smiled at him. His eyes had been open and staring at the ceiling, but at the touch of her hand he closed them.

A WEEK PASSED. Grey asked his father where the money should be paid. He did not trust him with so large a sum as was in the yellow envelope he collected from Eccleston's that morning.

He drove east on Highway 54, past the abattoir and pylons

and an unpainted concrete brothel to the hotel whose address his father had written on the back of the envelope.

The barman eyed Grey suspiciously then led him past bikies and off-duty police unloading the cash they could not bank into poker machines. The police and bikies sat shoulder to shoulder with retirees and pensioner women with purple-rinsed hair. Between the games they stared indifferently along with the pensioners at a television playing soap operas above the bar.

The barman told Grey to wait at the stairs. A girl with a broken lip and a closed eye walked down the stairs and into the night. The bartender came down and motioned upstairs with his thumb.

Grey knocked on a door and asked for Mr. H. That man was not in. Grey would wait. He waited an hour to deliver the envelope personally to a bald, well-dressed man with an untidy peroxide blonde on his arm.

"This is from Bill North," Grey said.

"Drink?' asked the man, turning his back to Grey and taking a bottle of cognac from his shelf. Grey had the feeling the man was modelling himself after a gangster from a movie.

"No thanks. Why don't you count the money?"

The man smiled warmly.

"Really, I trust you, boy."

"I've gone to the trouble of delivering it. You count it."

The bald man exchanged glances and smiles with the prostitute and another man in a pin-striped suit who Grey guessed was the accountant.

"If you knew me better, you wouldn't speak that way."

"I don't want to get to know you. I want you to count the money in the envelope."

The man snapped his fingers and the accountant brought out a red ledger then sat back down at the table.

While the man counted the money, Grey took in his manicured nails and trimmed eyebrows, then the vaguely masculine features of the blonde prostitute. Their eyes met. She looked at him dully and played with the gold bracelets on her wrist. Again, it was as though they were all acting parts in a movie. Grey felt like laughing. He felt absurd, sitting here above the pensioners who probably delivered the bald man as much money as his crimes. The scene was so juvenile and droll, but the danger was the child, the rich child who sat before him who did not see that this was a joke. Grey guessed he posed in the mirror before leaving the house, cried at the lyrics of popular love songs, but might shoot you if you laughed at his shoes.

"Correct?"

"Correct," said the man.

Grey stood up and left the room. He walked down the stairs into the bar and took a shot of Scotch then walked back into the ugly suburban night.

Another week passed. Then a month. The police investigation into the stolen horses barely existed. Some questions that were easily answered were asked of everyone within ten miles of the town. And no more was spoken by newspapers or men of the theft of horses from the property of a small-time Mary Smokes horse dealer.

# XIII

THE MARY SMOKES WORKERS' CLUB WAS A DIM-LIT THREE-
ply box attached to the backside of shops on Banjalang Street,
where the same beers that sold for three dollars at the hotel sold
for two.

Grey walked in and saw August Tanner sitting alone at a
corner table. Tanner never drank here; only poor boys, the
town's few Aborigines, and loose girls. It was the first time Grey
had seen Tanner since the night of the horses. Their eyes met
and Grey nodded. He felt an urge to go and talk, but he told
himself he must be careful not to be over-friendly, he must act
as he always would. Eccleston came in shortly after. He sat at
Grey's table with his back to Tanner. They drank beer and smoked.
They spoke of nothing out of the ordinary – hunting, horses,
and jokes at Raughrie Norman's expense – though their thoughts
were always with the man sitting at the other side of the room.
When Grey next went to the bar Tanner stood up too and sat down
with Eccleston. Grey heard the conversation over his shoulder.

"I had some work lined up for you the other day, Ook."

"What work was that?"

"Handlin some horses for me. Only they got stolen. You
heard about that."

"Of course. Shame."

"Yep. For you too."

"Why's that?"

"I reckon you could've used the money."

Grey turned to see Eccleston shrug dismissively.

"I'm used to not havin money. I can do without it."

Grey came back to the table with three shot glasses and half a bottle of Scotch whisky. Tanner nodded to him and took a glass and turned again to Eccleston.

"The four were just horses. But there was a black colt with em. That horse was worth more than you, Ook. Its blood was purer." Tanner sighed. "Well, now he's gone. How bloody complacent a man becomes. I should've had him in the stable. I thought the best place to hide a tree was in the woods. I was proud of that wisdom. And now all I can think of is some ignorant ringer usin him for a stockhorse, some cocky leadin his daughter round a houseyard on him. Well that just makes me–" he clenched his fist but stopped short of banging the table. He set his palm down gently. "I tell you, Ook. If I had've caught the son of a whore that did it, he'd've known he was alive – for about two minutes before he realized he wasn't anymore."

Tanner took a deep breath and calmed himself.

"So you owned em outright?' Eccleston knew the answer.

"They were mine. But not the black colt. It was necessary that horse should come through me, appear on my books. The vendor and buyer are both very difficult men to deal with. I tell you, Ook, the whole week after the theft I woke in cold sweats at the thought of explainin to em."

Perhaps Tanner had been testing him, but Eccleston's face had given nothing, and now it seemed like the old man only wanted to vent his worries.

"You've got insurance," Eccleston declared.

"For the horses. Not the colt. The colt was a dead racehorse." Eccleston raised his eyebrows.

"Disqualified," said Tanner. "Banned. Never to run again."

"How'd he die?"

"Irregular heart beat. It was all the chemicals they fed him."

"That'd do it."

"I tell you, Ook, the time and effort I put into changin that brand, a work of art it was, and all for nothin. When he was alive and racin he only had a little star on his forehead, and when he was stolen he had a full white blaze. That I did with dye and a razor blade. They couldn't a got a better man than me. And look how it turned out."

Eccleston recalled the horse now. The story had made the shire news-sheet; no doubt the papers in the city too.

"Perhaps you don't sympathize with me, Ook."

"I've got no love for horseracing – honest or otherwise."

Tanner sneezed. He pointed out the back door.

"West wind. I always get hay fever in a west wind. That wind was blowin the night the horses were stolen. I was bedridden. Couldn't hear anything. If not for that …' Tanner spat on the floor. "Keep your ear to the ground, Ook. You get around. You might hear somethin."

"I doubt it. Seems to me like they were out-of-towners."

"You never know. There are people round here in want of money. And the colt's not a horse anyone'd be likely to buy off the back of a truck – not for a hundredth part of his value. I got a suspicion they were amateurs."

"Maybe." Eccleston sipped his whisky. "How difficult are these blokes you're dealin with? You're a bastard of a man, always have been, but I'd just as well have you alive as dead."

"I don't know much about the vendor. The buyer – What I do know I suddenly hope isn't true. You've seen him. He was at my house the last time you broke horses for me."

Eccleston remembered the man with slick, thinning hair and dark sunglasses. Tanner knitted his brow and squinted and rubbed his grey chin stubble with visible pain.

"I'd buy the horse back if I could, Ook. I'd buy him back for twenty grand cash. I only tell you this so you can put the word out. Like I say, you know people."

Eccleston fixed Tanner's eyes.

"I don't know where your horse is, old man."

Tanner stood up from his chair.

"Well, I'll leave you boys alone."

Then he was gone onto the street.

"What do you think?' Grey whispered.

"I reckon it's crossed his mind," said Eccleston. "But he doesn't know. And we don't have to worry about the police. He would of rung em in a panic when he first saw the horses gone, but he'll be more scared of em finding the colt now than anything else. It'd raise questions the old man sure as hell doesn't want to answer. I bet he's been scolded by his associate for ringin em in the first place."

"What chance you think he knows?"

"He'd say if he knew for sure. This far on. I reckon he doesn't."

"It's goin on two months."

Eccleston nodded.

"Possum told me he's never got away cleaner. He drove all the way to Dalby. Sold the horses all to one man. He never had to leave a name, not even a fake one."

Grey breathed a sigh of relief.

He took up the amber bottle in front of him and filled both their glasses. Eccleston took the shot in a gulp.

"What's Irene up to tonight?"

"She's at home," said Grey.

"You know, Irene's—"

"Don't speak of her here, Ook."

Eccleston stared at him.

"Why can't I say her name?"

"Just not here."

"All right."

Grey went home and Eccleston stayed another hour by himself, taking straight whisky very slowly and deliberately at the bar until the bottle Grey bought was empty. Then he danced with a plump local girl and part-time prostitute. Then there was an argument with the bartender and he put his fist through a wall. Then he walked home alone.

WITHIN A FORTNIGHT Grey heard that the card game at Dinmore had packed up, for what reason he would never know.
Perhaps it had returned to the city. Oats and wheat were sown and
shot where sorghum had been. At dusk and dawn a burning
freshness filled the nostrils. The skies were higher. There was a
quickening of the breath and blood. And a day came when Grey
looked at the calendar in the living room and realized Vanessa was
back at school. Even in holiday time they lived far enough apart
never to meet by chance, and he had vaguely excused himself
from both her invitations before she left.

His days passed much as they ever had, running with the
boys of Mary Smokes in the forgotten town whose smallness
constricted their aspirations. Then one day late in May a wind
came and blew the long summer away for good. The wind
came from out of the inland and blew mares' tails across the sky
and swept and yellowed the grass and banished the rains so
the rivers and creeks became still and then dry, and then the lake
receded and left flats of cracking clay. A mist rose up from the
dry bed of Mary Smokes Creek like the ghost of water and drifted
through the eucalypts of the gallery. The old men said the creek
had dried earlier than ever this year. And as suddenly as these
changes in the weather, a day came when Irene did not wait for
him at the school gate. That day was followed by another. Then
she did not follow him around on Saturday nights or even annoy
him at the service station.

# Three

# I

GREY WALKED NORTH ALONG BANJALANG STREET. HE stepped off the asphalt for the speeding tourists who had come to use this road as a back way to the north coast from the west. He walked across the overgrown railway line, past unpainted houses with their front yards full of old stoves and car parts rusted by the rain. A shaggy pony with sweet itch and deep scratch marks in its hide leant across sagging wire to take what little green pick remained on the roadside. It was invisible at this hour, but at night, looking west, you could stand here and see the white haze of the new shopping centre's sodium lights. Parents took their children out of school to work there in the late trading hours, so this afternoon the town was empty.

Grey looked up and down the disused railway tracks, at the decrepit railcars where his sister and her friends sometimes played. She was not there. It seemed she had forgotten the arrangement they had made in the morning.

He sat in the gutter in front of the school and watched unknown cars go by.

He drove home. The boys were all standing on the road.

HOURS LATER, HAVING used up the town's bars, Matt Thiebaud, Raughrie Norman, Gordon Eccleston and Grey North walked down the midnight street with nowhere left to go but a half-mile beyond town to where they had hidden Grey's truck to avoid having to drive past the police.

Grey's birthday was gone and he had still not left town.
He kicked loose stones south along the road. They came to the
road sign that read "Mary Smokes. Inhabitants: 976." The sign
did not bother with any note of welcome. No one was stopping
here but those who called the place home. Thiebaud banged the
sign with his fist.

"Let's steal it," said Raughrie Norman, wisps of untended
hair blowing about his eyes in the dry cold wind.

"And do what with it?' said Thiebaud.

So they kept walking.

Grey had asked Bizzell for the week off leading up to Christmas in July. He looked inside the service station to see who was
taking his place tonight. A red-haired boy of about fifteen who he
did not recognize stood flipping through magazines on the rack.

In the pitching land just south of town woolly unridden
horses stood sleeping in defiance of the weather. A half-dozen
black-bally cattle picked grass around degenerate car bodies.

The iron skeleton of the drive-in movie theatre still stood
above town. The drive-in had been shut down in June. Even the
demolition job had been aborted, half-done. The canvas screen
was torn by winter winds. The poles that held the speakers for
cars still stood in lonely rows on the empty bitumen lot.

Grey's truck sat inside the drive-in's broken gates. It was
safer leaving it here than at the service station. The police were
awake to that. But the road tonight was free of police, and it would
not have mattered.

From the top of Solitary Hill the boys saw fires in a sweep
along the western horizon. Someone was burning raked timber.
From this distance and at night they could not be sure who. For
a time they all stood still, transfixed by the plain lit red.

Grey fell into the truck.

"Let's see if I can get my head straight enough to drive this
thing."

He pumped the accelerator to get the fuel moving and the

hundred-and-fifteen horsepower motor heaved into action, blowing heavy smoke into the cold.

They took a dark and winding back road on which they were unlikely to meet anyone.

They did not walk to Mary Smokes Creek tonight. Tonight the creek was a muddy trickle choked with weeds, and the water stank with algal blooms.

At home the yellow veranda light was on as he had left it, but all the windows were dark.

Eccleston walked to his own house. Matt Thiebaud lived at Helidon now to be closer to the new abattoir where he worked, so he would stay the night at Grey's along with Raughrie Norman.

Grey turned on the kitchen light and lit the potbelly stove and the boys sat down at the table. Bill North had taken a cash job fencing for the winter and Angela was spending the week with her sister, so Grey and Irene were alone.

Thiebaud put a cigarette in the stove pinchers and lit it in the flames.

"Where's Irene?"

"At Amy Minh's."

Grey looked at the clock on the wall that showed five minutes to one.

He took a mattress and blanket from the spare room and laid them down for Thiebaud and Norman in front of the stove. He threw a block of railway sleeper into the stove and stirred the coals.

"That'll burn through the night."

Raughrie Norman fell asleep as soon as he lay down.

"Irene comin home tonight?' asked Thiebaud.

"I doubt it."

"I'm glad. She might have seen this set up and reckoned me and Flagon were a couple of drunk queers broken into the place."

Grey smiled. The drink had worn off him and he did not feel like joking. He did not know where his sister was.

SHE CAME TREADING along the gravel way to the house. She opened the gate that sang on its hinges and stepped across the front yard wrapped in blue dark. She stood on the veranda while the west wind picked up and blew hard against the wallboards carrying smoke. She pulled back the hood of her duffel coat.

In his room Grey listened to his sister come in and kick off her boots. He heard the door of her room shut carefully, and through the wall he heard her pray the Hail Mary. After that there was quiet.

He had been sitting up in the house with Matt Thiebaud, but Thiebaud had gone to sleep an hour ago and now it was very late. He lay in bed and listened to the wind romp on the flats outside the house. He turned on the radio to a city station and listened to a performance of Bach's preludes and fugues that fell out and became static.

# II

GREY SLEPT UNTIL ELEVEN. WHEN HE WOKE, THIEBAUD
and Raughrie Norman were gone. He washed dishes and tidied
the kitchen to wake her and she came out from her room rubbing
her eyes.

He did not know why he did not ask her where she had been.
It was his right as her custodian. But he felt more anger than
was his right, and there were no words that would fit his anger.
So he was silent.

He sat on the front veranda and drank black tea and
watched the shadows of clouds glide across oats in the north.

Soon Amy Minh came by to take Irene to Mass. She did not
return until late that afternoon.

IRENE AND GREY drove into town to get fish and chips and
Matt Thiebaud sat down at their table. He had left his own car at
the garage and was looking for a ride to Helidon. Grey had
nothing better to do.

The three of them left the café with Thiebaud carrying his
dinner in newspaper. They drove to a service station and Grey
put twenty dollars in the tank and went to the counter to pay.
Irene got out of the truck to sit on the bonnet. A couple of boys
were filling up beside. One of them watched her. They were
out-of-towners. The one who watched Irene was a pretty, greasy-
blond-haired boy who Grey thought he recognized, but could
not say from where. Grey imagined the boy was eyeing he and his

sister in turn. Grey held his gaze and then the boy turned away to where the highway ran into the dark. Irene shivered in a T-shirt and hugged her arms into her chest. Grey watched the boy who smiled at Irene before he got in his truck and drove south out of town.

On the way to the big highway Grey delivered Irene home.

He and Thiebaud drove into the Darling Downs at dusk. The sky opened up. Starry and cold. The lights of cars and roadtrains flickered down the road. Runs of winter oats broke the miles of dry grass.

A biting wind blew through Plainlands where they sat drinking black tea at Rusty's Roadhouse cafeteria. Out the wide glass window were railcars loaded with coal. The railcars sat beneath sepia lights and ran far into the dark.

At Helidon derailed and graffitied railcars sat rusting beside a smoking, stinking abattoir and neglected football field.

"You should stay a while," said Thiebaud.

"I'd better get back."

"There's a game here tonight."

Grey looked down at the field that stole light from the glowing abattoir.

"We should have brought Ook," Thiebaud said. "Where is he tonight?"

Grey shrugged.

In truth, Grey had some idea. There was no more horse work, and Eccleston was back doing the same work he had skipped school to do as a fourteen-year-old boy: hunting and trapping in woods and scrub. He killed feral dogs, hares and foxes, though he could only collect a bounty on the foxes. He sold the salted fox pelts to a hawk-faced man at a pelt box for a few dollars apiece. The hares, he ate. The dogs he shot while contracted on a retainer by pastoralists or the DPI. Feral dogs were fiercer these days than they had ever been; his first contract came in autumn after a pack had carried off a four-month-old calf. The work meant Eccleston must be away, farther and for longer than he had ever been from his home, driving long hours alone.

Thiebaud slapped Grey's shoulder. "So you'll stay?"

Grey felt the cold bite his face when they were out of the truck. He took his duffel coat from where it was hooked over his shotgun on a mount behind the seats. He and Thiebaud stepped down onto the pitch where other hooded boys stood breathing smoke.

The rare game began and rolled on toward no foreseeable end. Grey was glad to be out of Mary Smokes.

BACK ON THE highway he remembered Vanessa. She might be in town tonight. It was a long weekend. He might stop in now before heading home. But he drove past the Haigslea turn-off. He wondered if she would have welcomed him.

The house was empty when he returned. He drove into Mary Smokes and walked by a military recruitment night at the Lyceum Hall. He stood by the window listening to a shaving-rashed major talk about duty and prosperity in the same breath. He walked north then south along Banjalang. There was nothing and no one on the street save the light of spare orange lamps and a couple of boys loitering in that light outside the Workers' Club. He put his head in the door of the club but saw no one he knew. He got back in his truck.

HE SAW A human shape on the side of the road in front of his house. As he drew closer, the figure became two. Eccleston and his sister. Grey imagined Eccleston had her by the arm. At fifty yards this was not the case. But he could not dismiss the notion that when he first saw them Eccleston had hold of her.

"I'm glad you're here," she said directly he pulled up. She did not give Grey a chance to ask questions. "We were walking home. But I'm tired."

"Get in," Grey said. He looked into Eccleston's eyes. He read some discomfort there, but he could not define it.

"You want to come to the house?' he said. "No one's home."

"No. Thanks. I'm goin into the hills early tomorrow."

Irene clung onto Grey's arm. She sighed deeply. Her black hair fell from her hood across her face.

"Take me home, Grey."

Eccleston stood with his head down in the dark on the road.

"What is it, Ook?"

"Nothin." Eccleston slapped the roof of the cabin. "Goodnight, Grey."

IRENE STOOD WAITING for him on the stairs. From the truck he watched Eccleston walk along the way to the big white house.

HE CHOPPED WOOD by the light of the moon with a bottle of beer. The beer ran quickly through his blood. In time Irene came and stood in the back doorway. He had been drinking and splitting blocks for some time before he knew she was there. He looked up.

"What's wrong?"

"Nothing."

"Do you want to go into the shed and get me a couple more logs?"

"Grey," she whispered.

He threw the halves of a split block on the pile. He waited.

"I'll get the wood," she said at last.

She returned with only one more block.

"Come in and sit with me," she said after he split the block.

He did so, but she did not speak for the rest of the night. He felt there was some significant revelation or question teetering at the edge of her silence. If once she had told him that someone pursued her against her wishes, if that was what this was, then he would have done anything to stop it. He wondered why she kept so silent?

She went to bed leaving him alone by the stove.

# III

GREY TOOK HIS BREAK-ACTION SHOTGUN FROM THE
mount in the truck and packed a box of rifled slug shells and
slung his leather water pouch over his shoulder and walked across
the grass to Eccleston's.

"North?"

"Ook."

"What are you doin here?"

"Day off. Last night you said you were goin into the hills. I
thought we'd shoot together."

Five traps hung on the bullbar of Eccleston's International.
He would usually take them off before driving through town, as
they made people nervous, but dawn was still an hour away. Grey
saw apple mint under Eccleston's stairs. A little garden of it,
cordoned off by smooth stones.

They drove onto Wivenhoe-Somerset Road and left the
truck on the northeastern edge of Lake Somerset. On foot they
followed a faint track through eucalypt woods and came into
dense forest on the old southern fall of the Stanley River catch-
ment. They walked up a creek called Gregor, high into the hills.
They drank stewed tea from Eccleston's thermos and water from
Grey's pouch.

There was a crackling of dry leaves and Eccleston set his bag
and traps down behind a tree and slung his rifle from his shoulder to his hands. The boys knelt in the brush. Eccleston imitated
the sound of a wounded rabbit and a red fox moved out of the

mist in the light timber. They stalked the fox up a gully and along a dry creek bed. The fox ran from scrub to tussock to iron bark. Eccleston had no dogs to flush the fox. He knelt on one knee for a quarter of an hour, fingering the inside of the trigger housing, then fired into a sliver of light between trees and shot the fox dead.

He laid his rifle on the ground and tied one of the fox's hind legs to a branch with a cutting of wire. He took his skinning knife from his bag and pushed the blade in above the left foot and cut across to the right. He skinned the fox and scraped the fat and gristle and stretched the skin higher up in the tree and threw the carcass to the birds.

They stayed in light timber another hour and the sun rose without trace of another fox or dog.

They walked high into rock ridges where no one ever walked and Eccleston untied a trap. He dug a hole with his hand. He rubbed his hands with eucalypt and kerosene leaves to disguise his scent. He kept an old shirt in his shoulder bag that he tied around his head so no drops of sweat fell on the trap. He bandaged the jaws of the trap with calico and dropped strychnine in between the folds. Then he placed a sheet of newspaper over the plate and hinges so the jaws would not jam on the soil. He set, laid and buried the trap but for a short chain and heavy metal drag. Then he went about setting the rest of the line.

"I'd rather shoot em than trap em," he said. "But we started too late and moved too slow."

Grey wondered if there was a note of resentment in the words. But Eccleston buckled up his shoulder bag with no particular expression on his face.

Resentment would have pushed Grey now, pushed him to ask about last night. Instead he kept silent. Anyway, it was for Eccleston to speak. Grey felt if he started it here and now he would likely burst into tears that reason could not account for, maybe even hit the boy who stood beside him. Eccleston must speak first if there was anything to say; otherwise they were finished. And they could never be as they were. But perhaps

Eccleston had nothing to tell him after all. Perhaps Grey was losing himself.

On the walk back, Grey sighted a dog in a fringe of cypress. They followed the dog along a dry creek bed but lost track of it. They sat down on an exposed tree root. Eccleston pulled back the bolt of his rifle to check the breech. He switched the safety and lay the rifle down beside him. He took Grey's water pouch up over his head and squeezed the bladder and let the water jet then trickle into his mouth. He handed the pouch back to Grey. Then he stared at his boots.

"You're my brother, Grey. My one true brother. But I wonder if you love me like I love you."

"What the hell's that mean, Ook?"

Eccleston stared at him and said nothing.

"Have it your way."

Eccleston laughed charily.

"You know you and Irene and the boys, but especially you and Irene, you're all I have in the world. I'm a broke half-caste who used to work horses and now shoots dogs." He spat. "You're a good man, Grey. But you don't know everything."

"What the hell are you talkin about, Ook?"

"Maybe nothin."

"Don't tell me that then tell me it's nothin. You're like a bloody child sometimes."

Eccleston nodded and rolled and lit a cigarette. Just then there was a cracking of twigs and the dog broke cover.

Eccleston slammed forward the bolt of his rifle and knelt on the floor of the wood. He pulled the rifle fast into his shoulder but the dog was already gone into the thick timber where they could not follow.

IN THE AFTERNOON Eccleston took his rifle and crossed Mary Smokes Creek and walked across Tanner's north country to Possum's humpy. He saw the bodytruck in the yard for the first time since the night of the horses. Possum must have borrowed it again from one or other of his cousins, who all claimed part ownership. The registration plates were gone.

Possum sat on the floor of the humpy with a bottle of whisky, watching a small television set. The boys had given him a hundred dollars of the horse money.

"And this is what you did with it?"

Possum grinned and pointed at the picture that rolled over and over like a reel of film.

Eccleston laughed and sat down on Possum's sour mattress.

"Let's go hunt some dogs."

"Why?"

"I need some money. You got any?' Eccleston smiled.

Possum shook his head.

"Cause you bin buyin whitefella things."

Possum grinned.

Eccleston looked on the floor and saw old pizza and hamburger boxes from Mary Smokes café.

"You bin eatin flash whitefella tucker too."

"If a bloke only et bush tucker e'd die."

"And now your money's gone."

Possum nodded.

"Come on," said Eccleston, standing up. "I set traps this mornin. I'll give you half a what's in em. Get your shotgun and a decent knife."

"Gun's in the truck," said Possum.

They walked behind the humpy and Possum climbed up into the cabin and reached behind the seat.

Eccleston rolled a cigarette and leant on the deck. He looked through the rails and saw halters tied inside. He saw dried horse dung.

"Pos."

"Yep."

The black man leapt out of the cabin with his shotgun.

"There's horse shit in the back a this truck!"

Possum furrowed his brow and nodded.

"You didn't clean the deck after we took the horses?"

"Nuh."

"And you left the halters tied ere?"

Possum looked embarrassed like a child.

"I left the number plates in a hole in the hills," he said. "Ownin halters don't mean nothin."

Eccleston looked away and spat.

"Where's this truck bin?"

"Lockyer for a couple a weeks. Then ere."

"How many blackfellas who know Tanner have you had ere since then?"

"Dunno. Few fellas from Cherbourg one night. But I don't reckon they know Tanner."

"Most of em have worked for im at one time or other. And Tanner knows you don't haul nothin anymore but whisky'n blackfellas' old furniture." Eccleston looked across the rolling country to the south. "Has Tanner bin round ere to hire you since that night?"

Possum thrust out his bottom lip and shook his head.

"E hired you?"

"No," Eccleston said. "Not once. And he's got unbroken horses too, and cattle to pull down from the hills." He sighed and wondered what that meant. At least Tanner had not been round in person and seen the truck. "Do you remember who you sold the horse to – the big one?'

Possum nodded.

"Like I said. Same as I sold all of em."

"Was e a dealer ord e keep im?"

Possum shrugged.

"Dunno, Ook. But I erd im say somethin about Ma Ma Creek."

"You reckon you could find im if you had to?"

"Dunno. Maybe."

Eccleston sighed and put his cigarette under his heel. He looked again to the south. "Get me a hose, Pos."

# IV

IT WAS THE NIGHT OF THE TIGER SCRUB CHARITY DANCE
and Irene walked to the truck barefoot, carrying her shoes in
her hands. Grey noted her blue-painted fingernails. Amy Minh's
Yunnanese mother had given her a high-collared *qipao* that she
had worn herself thirty years ago in another country. The woman
felt sorry for the girl who had no mother and was always with men
and boys and had no pretty things.

Tiger Scrub lay to the northwest of Mary Smokes, twelve
miles off the Valley Highway. It was not a town, but a cattle-graz-
ing district. One small yellow hall beside a schoolhouse was
all that marked it out from the surrounding country that was poi-
soned and ringbarked so dead trees stood pale and twisted on
the hills.

THEY LEFT THE truck on the gravel in front of the hall. They
came up the stairs where a small brother and sister sat playing
and already dirty-faced. The children smiled roguishly up at
Irene and she mussed the boy's hair. The smell of varnished floorboards came wafting from inside along with the pretty, waltz-time
music of a band.

The hall was powered, but the only electric lights were on
the stairs and in the kitchen and above the hole-in-the-wall bar.
Kerosene lamps sat on the tables and their light burnished the
walls. The band played on a raised platform in the corner before
a space for dancing where no one danced.

Grey looked over the crowd. The season's three showgirl entrants were selling raffle tickets. The boys were there. All but Eccleston. Irene spotted some of her schoolmates through a doorway on the back veranda and went to meet them.

Grey sat down next to Thiebaud on a bench along the wall. "Where's Ook?"

"Who knows." Then Thiebaud smiled. "Few out-a-towners here tonight. Look at her!"

He nodded in the direction of a girl in a slim-fitting red dress at a nearby table.

"Old Reg Swan's granddaughter. That's her parents she's with. She's all right, eh?"

Grey nodded.

"Why don't you go talk to her? You used to fence for old Reg, didn't you?"

"That was years ago."

Grey glanced again at the girl.

"I think I might have met her once."

"There's your ticket!"

Raughrie Norman crossed the hall in front of the girl, glanced at her, and came and sat down on the other side of Thiebaud.

"She's all right, hey Flagon?"

"Who?"

Thiebaud laughed.

"Why don't you ever wear your glasses out?"

"Who, Grey?"

"The girl in red."

"Oh, yeah. Yeah, she's all right."

Thiebaud laughed again.

"Don't try'n fool me, Flagon. You can't see a bloody thing from here. You're probably lookin at her father."

He put his arms around Raughrie Norman's drooping shoulders and the boy giggled.

"Go to hell."

"Her uncle looks all right from here too! Mind, I'm near drunk. You might be the better judge."

"Go to hell," Raughrie Norman giggled.

They were still laughing when Grey remembered very suddenly the thing he had forgotten and he felt a small hole – only the size of a marble – inside his stomach and he felt the breeze go through it though there was no breeze inside the hall.

"I'll be back in a minute, boys."

"Where you goin?' Flagon asked.

"Nowhere."

Directly he stepped onto the veranda the talking ceased. He glanced over the faces that looked up at him. There were four girls and two young boys he knew well enough. A boy shifted a stolen bottle behind a chair with his boot.

Irene smiled at her brother.

"What is it, Grey?"

He stood in silence, thinking of what to say.

"I was just wondering if you wanted something to eat."

"Are they serving already?"

"Soon."

She smiled and furrowed her brow.

"That's all right. I can get it myself."

He nodded and went back inside and sat down with Thiebaud and Flagon, feeling foolish and watching the front door while one by one the lamps went out and the room dimmed.

Thiebaud danced with most of the girls in turn. Raughrie Norman stayed faithful to the bench and the wall, looking around anxiously and tapping his feet in contemplation of a move that did not happen until dinner. Eventually Grey stood up and joined the line at the counter. The girl in the red dress lined up behind him. He looked over his shoulder and smiled at her. She stared at the chalkboard menu. She came beside him and stared so long and intently at the names of the three simple meals on offer that it was obvious she wanted to talk.

"Don't worry," he said, "the Women's Committee have never killed anyone with their catering, at least not in my time."

The girl smiled.

"You're Grey North, aren't you?"

"That's right." He was surprised she remembered him.

"I was at your house once with my grandfather."

"Yes, I remember you too."

He remembered her sitting in Reg Swan's car when the old man had come trying to recover a saw Bill North had borrowed without asking and then forgotten to return. That was six years ago. This girl had probably been too young to remember the circumstances.

"I'm Madeline."

He shook her hand. They each took a plate of fish and baked vegetables, and the girl took a bowl of bread and butter pudding.

"You can come sit with us if you like."

He could only accept.

She sent him for two glasses of Stanthorpe merlot.

Through the meal he watched the door. He felt no desire to make conversation with the girl beside him. Reason told him that he should. That was what young men and women did: talk politely over food and wine. He wondered what was wrong with him. Where was Eccleston tonight? He began watching the door without knowing who he was watching for, Eccleston or some other ...

His meal went cold.

He gave up watching. He felt ridiculous.

"So how long are you here for?' he asked Madeline Swan.

"Only until tomorrow night."

"Are you staying at Reg's?"

"No. At a motel."

He paused. He lost the thread of the conversation as a late arrival entered the hall. The vague shape of a young man transformed into that of a well-known old farmer.

"Which one?"

"The Pines."

Grey sighed. He stood up suddenly.

"Listen, why don't you and me get out of here and do something tonight?"

"Well ... I ... "

He had shocked her. He laughed at his audacity. Her easy manner of before was gone.

"I really should–"

"Forget it," he said. "We're backward this side of the hills. Forgive me." He sat back in his chair. "I was going to hit you with a plank of two-by-four as you walked out, but I thought I'd be polite." The girl did not take the joke at once. But Grey smiled and then everything was all right.

The meal was over. He excused himself and walked out onto the veranda and got a cigarette off Hart Bates. Bates did not talk and Grey leant on a post under a blue light and smoked in peace.

He felt a soft hand on his shoulder and turned quickly.

"I'm sorry about just then – if you were embarrassed."

"No."

"I guess you're mostly harmless," the girl smiled. She handed him a folded piece of paper. "This is my number. If you're ever in the city and want to hang out, give me a call."

He took the piece of paper and put it in the back pocket of his jeans.

"Sure. Thanks."

"Do you think you will?"

"Will what?"

"Come visit me one day?"

"Sure. Maybe."

"Maybe?"

"Without doubt."

Through the doorway he saw Irene had come inside. She was sitting on the bench next to Raughrie Norman who had only moved twice in the night. She smiled at her brother standing in the door. By the light of the kerosene lamps he noted the pretty blue dress whose foreign name he could not remember, the small Benedictine crucifix she wore on a bracelet instead of around her neck tonight, the elfin ears that showed through her blue-black hair that was perfectly combed. He excused himself and went in and sat down beside her.

Raughrie Norman was telling her about the fancy girl who Grey had sat with through dinner. Then he told her, if she wanted it, he would go to the bar and buy her a ginger beer. He was glad of her company. Sometimes the boys neglected him without thinking. She told him if he was happy to get it she would take a bottle, and he set off eagerly in the direction of the bar. He pushed his body gracelessly through the crowd waiting for drinks, determined to carry out the commission from the only girl in town who had ever treated him kindly.

She rested her head on Grey's shoulder.

"I saw you talking to that girl over there by the door. She seems nice."

"She is. She's from the city."

"She's pretty, don't you think?"

"No."

She smiled at him. It was late. It was late and whoever he was, he was not coming.

She took his hand.

"Will you dance with me?"

"No. I don't think so."

"Come on."

She pulled hard on his hand and he stood up and walked with her to the foot of the stage. The Ellis boys' band played a slow, plaintive tune led by violin. The long-bearded elder brother called the tune "Horses."

"What are you frightened of?' She put his arm around her waist.

He felt a stab of pain when he heard a woman's approving

voice from one of the tables, saying how decent it was of him to stick by his poor sister. The woman did not see the desperation gathered in furrow lines across his brow. Grey pressed close to his sister, but suddenly not too close. He opened his eyes and saw Raughrie Norman smiling innocently at him from the wall with a bottle of ginger beer in his hand, and his heart was eased. Then he saw the respectable people of town sitting at the tables and he felt hollow again. Then he closed his eyes and prayed that all that had troubled him of late was an iniquitous dream, a dream that would dissolve and all would be as it had been, and she would be his own small sister again, as she had always been, and he did not care who watched.

When the music stopped he clenched his fists to stop the trembling in his hands. Some of the diminished crowd clapped. Grey hurried off the floor and away from the applause without taking Irene's hand.

Thiebaud had danced with every girl and now all of them had left. He came over from the bar.

"I'm finished here."

"Why don't we go to the creek?' said Raughrie Norman.

"And do what?' said Thiebaud.

"Light a fire and drink. I got green ginger wine in your glove box. Remember?"

"It's too cold."

But there was nowhere else to go.

# V

THEY COLLECTED ECCLESTON FROM HIS HOUSE. HE WAS
sitting alone on the back stairs and staring at the road. They
walked to the bend in Mary Smokes Creek. The only water was
pooled in the deepest channel of the bed and tainted with algae.

The waters of the country were changing. Once, Mary
Smokes kept a little running water most of the year. These last
few years it was either dry or flooded. So much timber had been
pulled out of the high catchments in the north that streams'
headwaters had collapsed entirely, and when it rained broad
sheets of water fell down into Mary Smokes whose bed had
become full of bars and braids and gullies. Thousands of miles
of watercourses were lost. Instead of the old courses there were
newly cut flood channels, and a few old pirate streams like
Mary Smokes, where the rocks and timber lifted out of the bed
meant the water did not stay. These might threaten roads and
buildings given a great rain, but there was no water in them now.
Only those who walked the country knew these things.

Floodwater had gouged three extra feet out of this Mary
Smokes bend through the summer. The three feet were plainly
visible now the water was gone. Grey dreamt of dark water
rushing round here in the night with no one to see it. Many times
these last summers he had gone to the creek after a storm and
saw the water had bent and snapped steel railings on concrete
bridges; and when rain last fell in the west, the water in Mary
Smokes tore flood-level markers set six feet deep in limestone

clean out of the ground. And these things always happened at night, as though the water wished to keep itself secret.

IN THE WOODS they collected kindling and a couple of knotted eucalypt branches and made a fire. Eccleston was silent. The boys reckoned he must be drunk already. Flagon threw strips of bark into the fire that flared and crackled and died. The knots smoked sweetly for a long time before they caught and the smoke burnt their throats. The knots promised warmth through the night.

The bottle of Scotch that Eccleston had brought from his house was gone and they were forced to start on the ginger wine.

Thiebaud uncapped the bottle.

Grey watched Eccleston staring at Irene. Eccleston turned and met Grey's eyes across the fire. Then he said he had to check on Possum and stood up.

"You want a lift?' Thiebaud asked.

"I feel like walking."

He walked up the bank and out of sight.

Thiebaud turned to Grey.

"What's up with Ook?"

Grey shook his head.

They were near drunk now, all but Irene. She was going to Amy's house tomorrow for lunch and must not be sick. She had taken a half-shot of whisky and a ginger wine at the fire.

Raughrie Norman was asleep on his duffel coat and Thiebaud and Grey were talking about the girl at Tiger Scrub Hall and Irene was laughing at them when she shifted her feet beside her and her dress came up above her knees and Grey saw the long red scratch marks on her legs. The marks were made by fingernails, and he felt the marble-sized hole inside him grow wider and the wind come howling through it. Soon all the noise of the world was gone except that which came from the scratches on her leg and he thought, if it is going to be this way no matter what, if it is inevitable …

"Thiebaud," he said, without shifting his eyes from his sister. "Did you ever want to ruin a thing, so no one else could touch it?"

Thiebaud threw his cigarette into the fire and lay down.

"The drink's caught you."

GREY SINGED A strip of bark in the flames and let the wind tear at the ash. He sat up beside his sister. The other two lay asleep on the opposite side of the fire. He could see sleep and the little drink clouding her eyes. Quiet came off the plain and the dry creek. The eucalypt wood cracked and split apart with the heat. The splitting wood and the sucking fire were the loudest sounds in the night beside the quiet of the creek and plain.

"Irene, do you love me?"

"What do you mean? You're my brother. You're my best friend in the world."

"But," he dug the heel of his boot into the dirt, "do you love me?"

"Of course."

He sighed.

"Of course."

"What is it?' She put her hand on the nape of his neck.

"I just–' His face twisted with pain.

She smiled at him. She felt good amongst these boys who were so brotherly to her. She had been the centre of attention tonight at the fire. They would not treat any other girl so. If only she knew what he had done for her. You're spoilt, he thought. He did not smile back at her. He looked into the fire.

"You're spoilt."

"What's wrong with you?' she laughed. He did not answer. "Well, sulk then, you fool." She spoke loosely, tiredly.

"You think I'm a fool? Maybe I am, and in that case you can go to hell. Don't speak to me."

Tears came at once to her eyes.

"Grey? I didn't mean it."

Tears were in his own eyes but he refused to let them fall. He turned away to face the dark and he thought again of the long red scratches on her leg and his tears fell in rivulets before he even knew he was crying.

He was properly drunk now and the hard edges of the world had begun to fray and resemble the shifting fire. He felt reckless. He would twist the knife.

"You're not much, are you?"

"What?"

"You seem like something special, but you're no different than any of the others, than anything in this world."

She took his arm and held tight. He only stared into the fire. Her voice trembled. "Grey, stop it."

He threw his singed strip of bark into the flames. He whispered, "Irene, come with me."

"Where?"

He pointed to the dark of the cedars.

She followed him. She held his coat and sometimes his hand when she could not see. He stopped at a place where the fire was only a broken flicker and the sweet smell of the woods overcame that of smoke. He faced her. He put his trembling hand on her blue cheek, ran his fingers down inside her collar. She did not shy away … If she had it might have been possible. If only she would wince. The pale light brushed her pale, pale face and she was so beautiful tonight he knew he would die of it. He hated that anyone else should see it. He wished it were something he alone could see. And he knew he was alone, that nobody saw it but him. And he knew that everyone could see it. And still no one could but him. He was so tired. He closed his eyes and put his head on her shoulder and dreamt that the boys and the town were vanished, somewhere beyond the creek in the east, and that he and his sister were sitting in their house on the plain alone, and she was cold and there was no fire; and he lit a fire in the stove with the money he got working horses that day; and then to keep it burning he burnt all the money he made the day

before, then all the money he would make tomorrow, then all the
money he would make every day of his life; then he burnt bits
of timber he took from the house, just as he had seen Eccleston
do, and then all was alight, and the lacquer hissed and she
smiled at the beautiful colours; and then he made a fire for her
of the woods; and while the woods were burning he led her to
the bank of Mary Smokes Creek and he brought her a drink of the
water in his hands and they stayed there on the other side of
the water, on the opposite bank from the world, on the wide and
starry plain where the wind and the sound of rushing water
were their only companions and they needed no others, for every
speechless word she spoke was intended only for him and
intended only for this night where there was no future.

The wind rose and snapped a branch from a distant tree.

"What is it, Grey?"

"It's nothing. It must be nothing."

The cold wind tumbled down around their ears and rained
leaves on the ground and blew Irene's hair about her face.

He lowered his head so she might not see his tears.

"Grey, tell me what's wrong."

But he did not answer her. She sighed. She pulled up the
hood of her duffel coat and sat down on the floor of the wood,
looking now at Grey, now back through the trees to the fire. They
stayed there in silence.

She stood.

"I'm cold. I'm going back."

"Here."

He led her.

He stirred the coals.

"Get in close," he told her. And he put down his oilskin
jacket for her to lie on.

When she was asleep he walked back to his truck and
drove to town.

HE TOOK A drink at the Workers' Club then argued with a boy from Crows Nest. The boy brought Grey out onto the street and pulled his head down and landed two sharp elbows, one to the cheek and one behind the ear, and Grey fell bleeding to the side of the road. When he woke he sat down against the back fence of the hotel. By the time he realized he was too sick to drive home everyone on the street was gone.

He walked back to his truck. He sat at the wheel and looked across the street at a pane of broken glass held together with tape, at a smear of blood on the three-ply wall that was festooned with twinkling fairy lights. He wondered if the window had anything to do with him, if the blood was his own. He tried to remember what he and the boy had fought about.

I am not happy, he thought, as he sat buzzing-headed and watching the road. The purpose of life cannot be happiness. Else why, when I know things that would make me happy, that would make everything all right, am I driven toward things that will not?

He put his forehead on the steering wheel and put his hands together and prayed. Then he decided that that was not the kind of prayer God heard, even in His infinite pity. But Grey did not want that anyway. He did not know how to shape what he wanted into prayer or even into words. He fell down on the seat and slept until dawn.

# VI

HE SAT UP IN THE TRUCK WITH A FIERCE HEADACHE. He got out and leant against the bonnet and smoked and drank cold tea from his thermos. At the end of the dirt road the morning sun lit wild flowers and feathertop that grew up through the railway tracks. A palomino horse stood behind wire in a rectangular yard of the flowering grass watching him. He drove home.

HE RE-STRAINED THE wires of his back fence. He had no strainers and did the work with pliers, hitching doubled cuttings back around the fence posts, reefing on the wires, levering them around the old wire with the handle of the pliers. He cut his hands on the rusted barbs. At the end of the day three lengths of barbed wire still hung loose enough to be moved by the wind. He packed a forty-four-gallon drum full of nagoora burr, stick and an old tyre and lit it. He stood by the drum and watched Eccleston's horses make a game of running into the same wind that rattled his fence and moved the haying winter grass and twisted the flame in the drum below the pale sky.

He sat on the veranda and waited for Irene. The breath of the horses became smoke in the dusk. There was nothing to account for her absence.

He watched the road. He watched the land dim and turn a thousand nameless shades of blue and watched the lights of cars divide the dark until he could barely see. Then, just north of Eccleston's drive, a car slowed and sped off. Then there were two darkened figures standing where the car had been.

SHE HAD WAITED for him with Amy Minh at the restaurant. After that she had walked up and down Banjalang Street, hoping she might see him. At last she decided to walk home on her own. She was already out of town when she realized a blue truck followed her. The truck idled twenty yards behind and came no closer until she was nearly home.

She had been about to run when she saw Eccleston on the side of the road. Then the truck swung back onto the asphalt and sped away. Eccleston came from his house with the crowbar he had been using to lift a rotted post out of the front fence. He had seen the Holden truck and then seen what he thought was a young girl in its headlights. At a distance he thought the truck was Grey's. But then he thought about what had happened two nights ago, when a truck had sat waiting for her on the side of the road in front of his house.

He did not reach the road in time to make anything of the plates or the driver before the truck was only red tail-lights disappearing toward Highway 54.

So now they stood together on the road again.

"What are you doin out here by yourself?"

Her quickened breath broke her words.

"Walking home. Where's Grey?"

Eccleston looked across the way. There was not light enough to see Grey's movements from that distance, and there were no lights on in the house. Only the firedrum.

"Over there, I spose. Someone lit that fire."

Then he saw how shaken she was. Her hands trembled along with her voice.

He sighed and swore under his breath.

"Was that the truck from two nights ago?"

She nodded.

"It followed me."

"Was it the same boy? The blond one?"

"I've seen him before, but I don't know where."

Eccleston looked down the empty road.

"How long did he follow you?"

"Half a mile."

"Did he say anything?"

She shrugged and looked away.

"What did he say?"

She shook her head.

He sighed.

"Did the car stop? Did he try to touch you?"

"It didn't stop."

"I saw it stop, Irene."

Her eyes fell and her hair fell across her face.

"I didn't let him do anything."

"But he tried, didn't he? And last time too."

Eccleston grabbed her arm. He wanted her to tell him everything. His short breath made her think he was about to cry, though she had not seen him cry in all the fifteen years of her life.

He let go of her arm and gathered himself.

"Don't tell your brother. Not yet. He might take it to heart and do somethin stupid." Eccleston remembered the ten-year old boy who had taken on men in a human ring at Tanner's. He kicked a clod of dirt off the road. "I might too."

She nodded.

He leant toward her, to hold her. Then he stopped himself. He put his trembling hand on the top of her head.

"Leave it to me. But don't walk on the road alone. Don't leave the school ground unless Grey comes to get you. And if Grey's not home in the day, lock the doors of the house. And if he's not home by nightfall, well, you come to me."

He leant down to kiss her. She turned her face and let him kiss her cheek. He sighed heavily. "Go home."

He stepped off the asphalt and walked back up the way to his house.

HER FOOTSTEPS SOUNDED on the gravel. She came as far as the foot of the stairs and she still had not seen him sitting at the top of them.

"Where have you been?"

"Grey? God, you frightened me!' She did not let her eyes meet his. She walked past him. She took off her shoes. "At Amy's. I told you I was going there. And where did you go last night?"

"You walked home?"

"I had to. I was worried sick about you. Someone said you were in a fight?"

"You shouldn't be walking on the highway at night. It's dangerous. But then, maybe you didn't have to walk far."

"What do you mean?"

"I saw you out on the road with Ook. You think he's some kind of saint, don't you? You know, I've seen him beat hell out of a man for money. Stand by watchin horses caught in wire, tearin themselves to bits to escape a fire he lit. He spent the night in a whore's arms at the Workers' Club a month ago."

"I don't know what you're talking about," she whimpered without looking up at him. "But you're all right, and that's what matters to me. You haven't made dinner?"

"I was waiting for you."

"You're such a child. Why don't you turn a light on?"

He followed her inside and she turned on the kitchen light and lit the potbelly stove and she saw his face.

"What happened to you?"

She went to him and put her hands on his cheeks and ran her fingers over the wound.

"Don't touch me."

He caught her hands and threw them down. He had made her cry again.

"Grey, I can't stand this! Why do you hate me?"

"Because you're worthless. Because you're just as worthless as everything else."

"Grey, stop it. Please – "

He picked her up and sat her down on the table. He rucked up her skirt.

"What's this, Irene?"

She pushed the skirt back over her legs and hung her head and would not look up.

"It's not what you think."

"Why would you let someone touch you like that if you weren't worthless?"

She held her face in her hands. Grey's mouth twisted with pain.

"Why would you let a man hurt you? Why? Did he tell you this was love?"

He slammed his fist down on the table beside her.

His eyes filled with tears. It was painful with the swelling in his cheek.

"Tell me who it is, Irene. I know already. But you say it. Tell me and I'll right it. I'll deal with him. Men will harm you if you let them. You don't know them like I do. They don't know what you are."

Tears streamed from her eyes. Then from his.

"Tell me you want me to stop it."

He ran the back of his hand along the length of the cuts on her leg and leant his broken cheek upon hers.

"I don't know," she whimpered. "I don't know ... I don't know."

She caught his hand and turned quickly when they heard Eccleston's truck on the driveway. The white headlights came in through the kitchen window. Irene got down from the table and smoothed her crumpled skirt. Grey wiped his eyes with his sleeve.

Eccleston had driven the Valley Highway to Highway 54 and seen nothing. No sign of the blond boy and the Holden truck. When he got to the T-junction he got out of his cabin and looked east and west along a synthetic river. The lamps and glinting electrical pylons that kept sentry beside it seemed a parody of the Mary Smokes boys and their vigils at the creek. The blind watch of the highway lamps was ceaseless. Their light obscured the dark and the truths of the dark and even the stars. A road-train roared past. Then a speeding sedan that was followed by another. Eccleston sat down in the cabin and shut the door and turned his truck around.

And now he had pulled into Grey's drive.

Grey walked down the stairs to meet him at the firedrum. Eccleston's horses were huddled near the drum and shielding each other from the wind that was bitter cold now at the approach of night. Eccleston breathed smoke.

"I'm thinkin of going away for a day or two."

"What for?' Grey asked.

"Look for a horse."

"What horse?"

"You know what horse."

Grey glanced up at the sky, at the unravelling smoke.

"Don't be stupid, Ook. That's done."

"Maybe."

"What do you mean 'maybe'? Do you know somethin?"

"No. Just a feelin that we should get that horse back."

"Then leave it."

"Don't worry. No one can track me. Come with me, in case we have to steal him back?"

"No."

Eccleston sighed and looked into Grey's eyes and then looked into the dark and spat.

"Send Irene to stay with Angela in the city for a night or two and come."

Grey shook his head.

"Right now, worst comes to worst, we've got Tanner to deal with. I reckon we can handle him."

Eccleston nodded and stared at the firedrum, at a spark flung up to the stars.

"Then look after Irene while I'm gone."

Each fixed the other's eyes.

"I always do."

"I know."

"Have you got somethin more you want to say to me?"

"No. Nothin."

"You know she's a child, Ook."

Eccleston breathed deeply.

"I know. So I'm sayin look after her."

He turned and walked back to his truck.

Grey sat on the stairs and watched him go. He went back inside.

Later that night the telephone rang with an offer of work.

# VII

RUSTY'S WAS AN INDEPENDENT ROADHOUSE BETWEEN towns on Highway 54, and the only lonely accent on that nighttime stretch of plain. There were petrol and gas pumps in front, two diesel pumps on the floodlit dirt at the back, a kiosk and cafeteria, and a totem pole of neon lights hard by the road beaming "RUSTYS" – "24HOUR" – "89.9 CENTS" – "ROADHOUSE" into the dark.

At half-past five Grey was out the front stacking bagged firewood. The light failed fast behind him and when he looked up he saw faded blue day, copper dusk and dark night and stars in a line. A railways friend of his father who moonlighted at the roadhouse had left town for the weekend and needed someone to fill in his shift. Grey had worked at Rusty's twice before. He was glad of the excuse not to stay in Mary Smokes. He was glad to be alone.

A dozen roadtrains and twice that many tourists' cars invaded his solitude and for two hours together he was busy. At nine the cafeteria cook went home. She left fried potatoes, boiled peas and slices of roast beef in the hotbox and left the big auto-brew coffee pot full. She made Grey a toasted beef and mustard-pickle sandwich before driving off toward her waiting family. He finished the sandwich with sweet black coffee then swept out the cafeteria, hosed oil off the cement and stacked milk and bread crates out back on the graded dirt.

Soon there was nothing to do in the ever-lengthening

spells between vehicles but sit at a table in the cafeteria and stare out the window. He watched a ragged middle-aged man come down the road, suitcases in hand, and sit at an outside table without coming inside. The man had dyed-black, brylcreemed hair and wore grey pants and a tartan jacket with white-capped leather shoes. He looked like he had spent all his life living in motels and ten-dollar rooms above bars. In a while he walked to the edge of the highway and sat on his bags before the ash-grey plain. He waited a half-hour, eyeing the highway east, before a McCafferty's bus stopped and carried him away.

An hour passed and Grey saw no one else. There was a television mounted in one corner of the cafeteria and when boredom got the better of him he turned it on. He poured himself a black coffee and watched a black-and-white comedy to its end.

A bus stopped and delivered two boys who stood joking with each other on the concrete in the dry cold. When they tired of the cold they came in and bought cigarettes. They told Grey they were business students on holiday. Grey asked what kind of business. The boys laughed at the question. Then a horn blast issued from a late model sedan and the boys ran outside and were gone.

The clock measured another lonely hour and Grey made himself another coffee and smoked a cigarette. After midnight a buzzing, watery-eyed fatigue took hold of him. It felt like being drunk without the sense of wellbeing. It did not normally begin for hours yet. But he had been tired at the outset tonight.

Suddenly an old man was sitting at table in a dim-lit corner of the cafeteria. He was mumbling to himself and looking up every so often at the graveyard shift soap operas Grey had unintentionally left playing on the television. Grey sat down at a table next to the man and offered him a cigarette. The old man slid his chair across the floor and asked Grey what he thought about the war. He was not drunk. Not just drunk. Grey could tell he was crazy. An old man whose mind was too convoluted to let him sleep. Grey tried to figure out which war the old man was talking about.

"And I've still got me issue, elmet an rifle an all. They tried to take em off me but I kept em! I keep em in me ome. And a grenade too, undetonated under me bed ... "

But an unlikely station wagon pulled in for fuel and Grey had to attend it, leaving the old man telling the story to himself. The station wagon carried a small sleeping family. The wife was dozing in the passenger seat and three blond children were nestled in the back. The husband got gingerly out into the cold to fill the tank. Grey kept his eye on the old man through the cafeteria windows while he wiped the windscreen. The old man still sat at the table talking to no one. Grey sighed with a little envy at the family who seemed so out of place here this late at night, as though they had taken a wrong turn, driven here from some distant other world.

When he got back inside, Grey made the old man a coffee and a roast beef sandwich. The old man drank the coffee with a half-dozen spoonfuls of sugar but only toyed with the sandwich. He was off the war now. He was talking about something else, but Grey could not make it out. The air became cold even in the cafeteria and Grey went out to the truck to get his jacket.

When he returned the old man was gone.

At half-past eleven Grey watched a lime-green Datsun Bluebird pull in and sit spluttering on the concrete before it was thrown into gear and jerked forward, cutting the motor. Two boys got out rubbing their necks and laughing. Grey knew them. They were a pair of contract fencers. A thirty-year-old simpleton called Jack Harry and a raw-boned kid called Skillington, both from Haigslea. "Only way you can stop it is stall it," said Jack Harry. He slapped the Datsun's roof.

"Where are you headed?"

"We're at a party at Lockyer. We're the supplies bus. No one on this whole bloody highway's open except you."

"What about the Sundowner?"

"Nope. You got any ice?"

"In the freezer by the door."

"Cheers. What kind of booze you have here?"

"A couple of bottles of port and boxes of goon. That's all."

Jack Harry sent the Skillington boy for the wine and ciga-rettes. He went himself for ice. He took three bags and put them behind the driver's seat and leant on the car while Grey cleaned off the windscreen.

"How much for those?"

"Twelve dollars."

"Bloody hell!"

"I don't set the prices."

The Skillington boy came out with a bottle of port and a box of cheap Riesling, a litre of ginger ale and a pouch of tobacco.

"All that's thirty-three fifty. Plus the ice makes forty-five."

Jack Harry handed Grey two twenty-dollar notes and looked apologetic.

"That's all you've got?"

"That's all I've got."

"It'll get taken out of my pay when it comes up wrong tomorrow."

Skillington went to the car and scratched up a dollar twenty. He handed it to Grey and Grey sighed.

"All right."

"Thanks, Grey. You're a mate."

He took the money and walked back toward the kiosk. What did he care about the money? He laughed at himself.

Jack Harry called out to him.

"Hey, Grey! Vanessa Humphries is back in town. She asked about you tonight. I'll tell her we saw you."

"Thanks."

Grey was surprised she had even thought of him. He had not seen or heard from her for months.

He put the money on the counter, and Jack Harry stuck his cowboy-hatted head around the door.

"Grey, you couldn't give us a hand startin the car, could you?"

"What's wrong with it?"

"Don't know. Just won't go."

The Skillington boy stood beside it on the concrete looking helpless.

Grey sat down in the driver's seat.

"It's a moody old bitch," said Jack Harry.

"Is it yours?"

"No."

Grey turned the key and the motor only wheezed. He shut the door.

"You boys push me," he said through the window. "Push me onto the road."

He held down the clutch and the two boys pelted onto the roadside with the car that ran away from them and stuttered and fired and Grey pumped the accelerator and shifted into third gear.

The highway to the east and the city lay before him, the road to the long-threatening, long-overdue future. In the rearview mirror he saw the two hopeless boys, silhouetted against a roadhouse that had forty-odd dollars lying on the counter and another four or five hundred in the till, and he thought about leaving them with it and keeping going.

But he turned the car around.

AFTER AN HOUR a police car stopped and two officers stepped up to the kiosk. One fiddled with his holster and leant sideways on the counter.

"There's been a report of a stolen vehicle, most likely headed in this direction."

"Which direction is that?"

"East out of the Downs. A green Datsun Bluebird. I don't suppose you've seen it?"

Grey smiled. Likely as not the police had driven past it on their way to here.

"Sorry."

"Something funny?"

"No."

The officers walked back to their car with no more said.

The stolen car probably belonged to some kid's parents, and when the kid saw it gone from the same party Jack Harry and Skillington were at he must have panicked. Jack Harry would have gone looking for any vehicle with the key inside and taken it for fun, for boredom. Grey laughed. He would not have gotten far tonight. They were chasing him before he even ran.

He stared out the window. A west wind blew leaves across the lit concrete and into the dark.

He took out his wallet and palmed the photograph he kept of his mother standing in the yellow grass in front of their house. He smiled at her hair in pigtails and the big pink coat that made her look so young. He was already nine years older than she was in the photograph, in a year he would be older than she would ever become. Tonight he could not remember her voice or even a single word she had spoken, yet she seemed close to him. She belonged to him much more than she did to the young man standing beside her, looking much like himself, who would right now be drinking away these hours before morning in the solitude of some outback hotel room. Yet without the photograph Grey could not recall her. There was a spirit who inhabited his dreams; it felt like his mother, but he could not be sure. After a time of staring, the photograph recalled his sister. The sad mouth paired with exuberant eyes. He put the photograph away and walked out into the night.

The three o'clock highway ran silently through the grassland and through grey fields that were mostly fallow now. At the eastern entry to the roadhouse was an eternally empty noticeboard to advertise goings-on in nearby towns and Grey leant against it. The Milky Way stretched farther and brighter than he had ever seen it and the sky was washed out with dirty twinkling.

He switched off the inside lights and the neon criers at

the main and sat down on the gravel by the road, and then he and the roadhouse were lost to an oblivion of stars and plain. He thought that the dark that enveloped the land was the same that God divided on the first day, and it had not grown a moment older or changed, no matter how many lights men shone into it, and in that eternal dark nothing was certain. Grey wondered where she was tonight, if she was with he who he had loved since boyhood – or was it some other after all? It was better to have no idea. It was better like this, out here away from it. He tried not to think of her and instead he thought of Vanessa. He wondered how long she would be in town. She had asked about him tonight. Perhaps he had been unkind to her, been foolish. Again tonight, far out in the west, the land was burning. The fire nipped at the southwestern stars and held him. Then he thought of her without being able to help it. He spoke her name to the dark, to the empty distance between himself and the heavens. At times God seemed on the verge of speaking across that distance, but the word was always withheld, or was whispered and not understood, and he wondered was the universe holy and meaningful, as the ancient saints had it in his mother's books, or was it all just a tawdry, banal and violent nothing, like this highway, where the pretty glare of lamps made the earth a depthless plane.

It was six o'clock. A red front stretched the length of the eastern horizon to counter the front in the west. The western front retreated and failed in a haze of smoke. He sat before the roadhouse with his eyes closed and his head between his knees below the ever-fading remnants of last night's universe.

ECCLESTON SAT ALONE IN HIS HOUSE. HE HAD TALKED with Possum through the afternoon and marked the place with pen on a road map. Now a candle sat on the windowsill and he watched the jumping flame. He looked for the hundredth time in the night across the way to the North house. He saw her in one of the lit windows. Then the lights went out. It was very early morning. He watched the candle twisting and the wax burn down and the flame glow and glow and then go out with a ribbon of black smoke. He got in Possum's bodytruck and drove out to the big highway and drove west.

# VIII

THE NEXT NIGHT GREY ATTENDED THE SHOWGIRL'S
crowning dance with a vague hope of seeing Vanessa. He scanned
the hall for the boys but they were nowhere amidst the small
crowd. With a fifteen-dollar cover charge and no beer at the bar,
he reckoned they would not be coming. He had asked Matt
Thiebaud who had given him a doubtful "maybe'. He could not
see Vanessa either. She had attended this party in years gone.
But why should she be here tonight? He took a glass of red wine
and laughed at himself. He nodded to Jack Harry, who would not
be here but for his plain young cousin who was one of the showgirl entrants. Grey decided to finish the glass and leave when the
voice he recognized spoke close to his ear and her hand fell on
his shoulder.

"So they've let you out, have they?"

He smiled at the meaningless quip. She was smiling too,
that credulous, indiscriminating smile that lit her face like
a ray of warming light. He realized what a long time had passed
since he had seen her. She gave him such physical relief that he
sighed and breathed deeply, as though a weight had been lifted
from his shoulders. She had lightened her hair and it hung
loose over her ears and touched her neck, and the kerosene lamplight showed her skin to its fullest golden hue. She was beautiful.
Grey remembered her birthday had passed since he had last
seen her. Even in those months she seemed to have grown up.

"You must be twenty-two now."

"Twenty-three, Grey. You don't remember anything, do you?"

He remembered their first kiss. They were sixteen and thirteen and she had just taken her first drink of blackberry wine. He had stolen the bottle from his father's cupboard. It was the sweetest-smelling thing he could find and she said it was blissful and felt a little like cheating, drinking alcohol that tasted so good. He remembered the excitement of having a girl, of her already swollen body that made his loins sing with a strange pain, and the way she spoke and held his hand that seemed so wonderful and grown up. That was the night he decided to marry Vanessa Humphries. He knew he was only one of a number of boys she had played at love with. Even so, he always felt he had the edge on the others, that when she had exhausted them she would return to him, or somewhere within arm's reach of him, and they would pick up where they had left off, and he had long been justified in this feeling.

"So how are things?' she said. "I haven't seen you for so long." She spoke without any of the awkwardness or spite he had been prepared for, that he thought his inexplicable disappearance from her life deserved.

"I've been around. What about you? How's school?"

"Only half a year to go. It's very exciting."

He nodded. He imagined kissing her tonight, sneaking away laughing into the dark, climbing into one of the rooms of the schoolhouse beside the hall.

"No big news then?' he said.

"Well – I've gotten engaged."

"Oh." He felt cheated. "When?"

"A couple of weeks ago. It happened quite suddenly."

He stumbled over his words that he saw made no sense: "I'd been meaning to call you."

They looked at each other with embarrassment until, unable to hold her gaze, he glanced away across the room at the blurred faces of the crowd.

"Now don't pretend you were ever serious about us, Grey."

He sighed.

"Why not? Who is he?"

"You don't know him. His name's Michael Reed. He works on a newspaper in the city. He's just over there. He and his family wanted to see where I grew up."

Grey looked across the room and found the tall man she pointed at. He was talking with a smartly dressed woman who bore sufficient resemblance to him to be his sister and who was cradling a child.

"Your mother must be happy."

"She is. Though she'd be happier if it was going to be at the Presbyterian. Michael doesn't want a church wedding."

Grey nodded. He saw the chain around Vanessa's neck now bore a heart-shaped locket.

"Come and I'll introduce you!"

"In a minute," Grey said.

And all at once he was not talking to her anymore. She had said goodbye and walked across the hall. He lost her in the crowd. He saw her next standing at the edge of the dance floor with her fiancé's sister, having relieved that woman of her child. Vanessa rocked back and forth and side to side, lulling the child in her arms to sleep, her figure hinting at itself as if by accident through her pretty beige dress. The child was not hers, but to see her cradling an infant on her hip, where her own would be after a few short years had passed him by, hurt him.

Later he spotted her alone in a corner of the hall. He went to her and caught her hand and held it. He could see the discomfort it caused her, but he did not let go. This – Vanessa and all that went with her – was real and good. If he could hold onto it he might make something real of himself also. So he kept hold of her hand despite her protests.

"No, Grey," she whispered, her eyes darting around the room, "I can't."

"Is he giving you trouble?' said a red-faced young man in a sports coat who was even drunker than Grey.

"No, Tommy. I'm fine."

Vanessa pulled on Grey's arm. She scowled at him and pulled free. He walked out to the car park and stood alone next to his truck without getting in. He sucked the cold air in long draughts until he was almost sober. Then he stood shivering in the blue light at the top of the hall's stairs for everyone to see. She went out to him.

"Why don't you go home, Grey? You're tired," she took his hand, "and look, you're cold."

Her fiancé came out to them.

"Who's this?"

Grey ignored him.

"That's the one I told you about," said the sports-coated drunk who joined the miserable party on the veranda. "The one who was giving her trouble before."

"Get out of here." the fiancé said. But Grey did not move or stop staring at Vanessa. "I mean it. Get the hell out of here, you dumb hick!"

Grey ran his hand over his face and laughed.

The fiancé thought it was at him. He pushed Grey and Grey tried to hit back but missed and fell backwards down the stairs. The next he knew, he was lying in the car park and the fiancé was kicking him on the ground and Vanessa was screaming for it to stop. Grey managed once to get to his feet and was knocked straight back down.

He sat on the dirt against a car wheel with a buzzing head. People were talking all around him but he heard nothing they said. Then someone had their arms around his shoulders. Then he was sitting in the back seat of Vanessa's car watching the fiancé where he stood on the veranda of the hall. Grey was dazzled by the headlights of cars that were pulling away, carrying people to the showgrounds and the melancholy annual cabaret.

AT THE SHOWGROUNDS Grey felt better and apologized and

even thanked Vanessa for the lift. Vanessa was crying into her hands.

He saw Matt Thiebaud sitting on the grass, listening to the band.

"You look like hell!' said Thiebaud.

"Thanks for showin up at the dance."

"I was goin to. I'm gettin bored with this here anyway."

"Let's go somewhere then."

"Where?"

Grey almost suggested heading north to Kilcoy, but then he remembered they were not welcome in that town on account of Eccleston's last trip there. He did not want to go back to the bars and poolrooms in Mary Smokes.

So they stayed where they were.

The band played on a truck deck. The steel guitar, squeeze-box accordion and violin played a long and ebbing tune. The crowd was thin and scattered. Thiebaud and Grey sat up close to the truck. Grey watched the bonfire beside the trailer, children skirting the edge of the flames. A small boy poked, touched, pulled away with too hot hands, then grabbed quickly and held a bit of wood burning at one end and circled the fire letting sparks fly behind him before throwing the wood back. A merry-go-round turned at the edge of the plain.

"What are we doin here?"

"What do you mean?"

"In this town." Grey breathed deeply and closed his eyes. "I'm twenty-five years old."

"We're makin our way."

Thiebaud took out his pouch and pinched the tobacco and rolled Grey a cigarette and then rolled one for himself.

"But I know what you mean, Grey. I know what you mean, all right."

So they both felt it tonight. Their tribe, the wild boys of Mary Smokes, was failing so suddenly.

"What have we been fighting against?"

Thiebaud looked into the dark. The burning end of his cigarette glowed against the outskirts of town that might as well have been the beginning of a howling waste.

"I don't know," he said.

What they had been fighting was uncertain, but both boys knew that somewhere in the night, even at the asking of the question, they had lost something unnameable and irrecoverable. Time overflowed with lost tribes. Why should this one of a half-caste, a simpleton, two poor boys and one's arcane young sister be different?

The band left the stage. The boys' sad reverie was broken by the end of the music.

"Where's Ook tonight?' said Thiebaud.

"Where is he ever, lately?' Grey drew on his cigarette. "Did I tell you I'm thinkin of moving to the city?"

"And that you were goin north to get work on a trawler."

"Did I say that? I might do. Next year."

"I don't much like the idea a workin three months straight."

"I wouldn't mind."

"You don't mind now. Wait till you've been doin it for a month."

"You're just lazy, Thiebaud."

"That's true."

They sat quiet again, listening to the bonfire. Talking about future plans with someone who believed in them made Grey feel a little better, and the emptiness inside him grew smaller.

"It's town's big night tonight, isn't it?' Thiebaud said.

"And tomorrow night."

Thiebaud dug a hole in the ground with the heel of his boot.

"But I know what you're sayin, North. Tell the truth, I am gettin sick of this same old thing year after year. I feel it most now in the winter."

Their home was sedated through the long months of summer. It slept and dreamt, waking suddenly in May when the air was filled with expectation and the chill promise of escape.

Grey wondered what would happen to Raughrie Norman if
he and Thiebaud left town. He mentioned this. The two boys
decided Eccleston would never leave Mary Smokes.

"Same work and no work, same people, same joints every
year," said Thiebaud. "Runnin round here after whatever girls
haven't moved away yet. I'm leavin town, all right. Get myself set
up a bit." He took a long drag of tobacco and blew it out the
corner of his mouth. "One day we'll all be set up, you see. You will
and I will, and even little Irene will."

Thiebaud could not hold Grey's gaze. He looked away,
then back at his friend, and then Grey knew that he knew; that
the secret of his sister was no secret at all.

"I think Ook loves her, Grey. I don't say that's right or wrong.
But then he told me he found her on the road the other night
talkin to some boy. Probably some poor kid from school. I don't
know who it was, but I think Ook might. Last I saw him he told
me he was sortin it out. So perhaps he's leavin her alone."

"He should have told me."

"I think he wanted to."

"And she … Does she –?' He turned his eyes to the ground.

"I don't know. She's strange, Grey. You know that. Once
Ook thought she did. But she told him some other had made her
a promise. Probably the boy he caught her with. I spose kids
make promises to each other all the time. You shouldn't be surprised. She's the prettiest girl anyone's ever seen. Someone was
bound to fall in love with her one day."

Grey shut his eyes and sighed deeply.

Thiebaud put his hand on Grey's shoulder.

Grey wondered who the boy was. At once he felt the need
to drive home and secure his sister and then find Ook and go
wherever was necessary to put an end to this. But then he let it
pass. There was nothing to do but let it pass. There was nothing
to do but accept. Despite her solemnity and strangeness, she was
a child, at times a childish child; just a girl who would one day
be a woman. And the other? Some poor rosy-cheeked boy in her

class at school who had spoken to her gently, or even if it was Eccleston she cared for most … Either way, a boy she admired. Someone who treated her as a regular girl: the daughter of her father; the possession of no one but herself. He felt guilty. So guilty he convinced himself he must be satisfied without knowing who the other was.

Thiebaud put his arm around Grey's neck and shook him.

Though he could not force a smile, Grey felt someway pacified. What had been happening with her these last weeks, this must be the natural way of things. It must be. And there was nothing truly wrong. It was a girl's right to grow up, however awkward and ungentle the process might seem. So he had been inventing it all. That part of him that had been growing into the monster in the woods and at the house with her, that wanted to fight against everything no matter what damage it caused, that part was burning him out so quickly. And that was what they called childishness. There was comfort in the knowledge it would eventually pass. The world would forgive him his youth, so long as he outgrew it. Now he must harden himself to a new degree to be equal to his inheritance.

THIEBAUD DROVE HOME and Grey walked the minuscule sideshow alley by himself, wanting to hold onto the armistice in his heart a little longer. After he had walked the alley twice and there seemed nothing he could do to prolong the night, Jack Harry came and slapped his back.

"Guess what I just saw?"

"What's that?"

"Vanessa Humphries and that bloke who hunted you outta the dance hall before. Over there behind the marquee near the sideshows. And he starts tryin to press her up onto the wall of the thing and she hit him! How about that, eh? Bloody hell, did she hit him!"

Grey smiled.

"It's just coquetry. She's playing."

"Hey? Nah, nah, she hit him. Did she hit him! Anyway, that's just deserts. Son of a whore. Comin to get a beer?"

"I've been drunk once already tonight. The second time's no fun."

Jack Harry shrugged and left him, and Grey decided to take one last wander about the night's diminishing entertainments. Anticipation had taken hold of him and was spoiling his peace. Without admitting it to himself he was looking for her. He found her standing before a stall of grinning clowns and grotesques. Under the stall's orange light a showman watched her little brother place ping-pong balls into the mouth of a clown. When the balls were gone the boy turned around pleading. Vanessa forced a tired smile and gave him a handful of coins to play again. She looked very sad. She saw Grey and sighed and looked down at her shoes and then took her brother's hand.

"Come on, Billy."

Grey followed her off the sweet-smelling sawdust, out of the alley and through the horse floats and caravans where wood smoke hung above the cold flat. They were back behind the closed pavilion in the dark, the place where she supposedly hit her man. She stopped and they stood staring at each other. She let go of her brother's hand. She turned around and looked like she was going to cry.

"Why are you following me? You're making yourself ridiculous, you know. There are plenty of other girls around. You don't have to come chasing me like an old dog."

Then she pursed up her little face and cried and could not be tough or proud or dignified anymore. She reached for his hand.

"Come on then."

They went out onto the highway and walked to her car.

AT HOME IRENE was asleep at the table with her head on her arms. She must have been very tired as she did not wake when Grey came in. It was dark but the embers in the stove glowed and he stood still and stared at her sleeping face. The night before, the mere sight of her was enough to pull his chest tight like a drum and make his insides hollow. But lying here now … he told himself she was just a girl, his sister, but a girl like any other. He noted her long greasy hair, pallid skin and stick thin arms … the tears that stained her cheek. These were capable of breaking his heart if he let them. Why, he wondered, have I only ever loved the small, the weak, the estranged: his worthless father, his suffering mother? Perhaps that was unnatural – one of those things he must change. And he felt he could change it. His heart had already become easier. Before it had burned with dark fires that promised neither light nor warmth and never let him rest.

He wondered if she had waited up for him tonight. Perhaps she had waited to tell him the thing that until very recently he had most wanted to know. The thing he had made so tremendous for her. It could wait now, he thought.

"I'm sorry," he whispered in her ear while she slept. How I must have wounded her heart, he thought. How I might have – He dared not think. He felt pressure leaking out of him like fluid draining from an infection.

He went to the sink and ran a glass of water and went to his bedroom without waking her.

For the first time in months he did not dream of his mother or his sister: those dreams without words that haunted his nights and left an uncharitable ocean residing in his heart. He was amazed at how tired he was. So tired he thought he might shut his eyes and never wake, at least not for the longest time.

THE BLACK MAN ECCLESTON HAD MET IN THE BAR PULLED off the highway ahead of him and pointed down a dirt road. Eccleston got out of his truck and walked to the black man's window.

"Half a mile down. Over the creek."

Eccleston nodded. Then the black man drove off.

He waited on the side of the highway and smoked while the night deepened.

He rolled down the dirt road in the dark, idling when he could and without headlights.

He crossed the dry creek on foot and stood in a gully beside the fenceline. Three hundred yards distant were horses. He crawled through the fence and walked across the flat. The horses stirred. He got close enough to see the smoke of their nostrils, close enough to see the smoky-black thoroughbred colt standing above a white mare.

He whispered under his breath, "Damn it, Grey."

He drove back to the highway hotel where he was staying and dialled the operator and asked for August Tanner of Mary Smokes.

"I know where your horse is."

Tanner spat down the phone.

"I knew it. You filthy black son of a whore—"

"Shut up, old man. I can get him to you in two days."

"Bring him tonight or there's trouble."

"There'll be no trouble. You listen. There'll be no trouble. You'll have your horse in two days."

"Get him here by tomorrow."

"I can't. I need another man."

"You bring him tomorrow." Tanner's voice trembled.

"What's wrong, old man?"

There was no answer but Tanner's troubled breath.

"What's wrong?"

"There's a boy been hired."

"What?"

"By tomorrow night it'll be too late. That's all I can say ...'

But Tanner stammered on. "There were signs, reasons, that made me reckon it was you and North. Then my client started puttin the screws on me. He knew I wasn't tellin him everything I knew."

"What boy's hired?"

"My client's picked him out. My client's comin round tomorrow night. I had to be seen to be doin somethin, Eccleston. You pushed me too far." The old man sounded close to tears.

"You damn fool, Tanner. Call him off."

"You don't understand. I've held him off this long – held him off as long as I could. But I don't know where he is. I don't even know his name. You bring me that horse, so I can ring my client and promise him he can come round and see him tomorrow. He alone'd be able to call the boy off now."

"I've seen the horse. I saw it tonight. I can tell you where to find it. And I can get it for you the day after tomorrow. Ring your bloke with that. Be reasonable, you bastard."

"The men I'm dealin with aren't reasonable, Eccleston. This isn't a reasonable world. Just cause it's in one place tonight, that horse might be gone by tomorrow mornin, gone without a trace. You should know that." Tanner paused. "I'm glad I got this chance to warn you … But the boy … I'll make sure of it … he won't–"

"You don't know what the hell he'll do."

Eccleston slammed down the receiver. He dialled the North house but there was no answer.

He drove back down the highway, back down the dirt road. He hid the truck as best he could in the trees. He reckoned this was the only road out of here. He pulled dry stick and logs up over the road at a gully between the creek and his truck and doused them with fuel.

He took his pliers and a halter from behind the seat and cut the fence at two posts and threw fifty feet of barb on the unlit bonfire in the gully and walked to the back of the paddock where the horses were. He checked the wind and poured petrol after his steps until his jerry can was half-empty and poured the rest along the creek and he threw the can into the bed.

On the other side of the creek was the house. One blue bug light swung on the veranda in the rising west wind.

He squatted on one knee and whistled and the horse's ears pricked. He clicked his tongue and whistled as quietly as he might and looked in the colt's eyes and then looked away, and the colt came. Eccleston shifted close enough to stand and get the halter over the colt's head. " You remember me," he said. But he stood on the lead rein and tripped and the horse spooked and squealed and the lights came on in the house behind the creek and men's voices shouted into the night. He kept hold of the horse. He wrapped the rope around his elbow and hand and pulled the horse toward the road and heard an engine and closed his eyes. The car would come around on the road but men might walk across from the creek. He wrapped the rope around his hand again and knelt in the grass and struck a match and lit where he had poured the petrol. The dry grass caught and the fire began to run in an arc that would shut the creek off to men on foot. He threw another match when he was halfway across the paddock and another at the fence. He dropped his cigarette lighter into the pile of deadwood, wire and brush that he had blocked the road with. He heard a man's voice cursing down on the creek and then the crack of a rifle shot. The colt was spooked by the shot and by the fire and tried to pull free, but the rope was wrapped twice around Eccleston's hand and elbow now, and his arm would break before he let go. The car skidded just the other side of the fire on the road. He swore at himself for not having dropped the ramp of the truck. If only the ramp was down and the engine running; if only there was a driver at the wheel to press the accelerator to the floor when he loaded the horse and flung himself after it. But that was a foolish dream. He was all alone.

A man's voice swore and told him to stop where he was. He was thinking if he could just pull the ramp down and load the horse he would be safe when another rifle shot cracked the air and he felt a thump in his chest like a horse's kick and fell on his back and put his hand on his chest and he could not believe there was so much blood. He could see the horse shivering at the edge of the fire, the rope dragging on the ground. He went to get up and re-catch the colt and realized he could not move, or per- haps he was too tired to, for he did not feel any pain. Then the horse was gone and even the fire and the men's voices were gone and there were only the stars and the starlight, roaring like a river in flood above him …

THE MEN DRAGGED the body further along the gully into a ditch in the dry bank of the watercourse that was the farthest western stream that ran into a little-visited creek in the Brisbane Valley called Mary Smokes. There was no water in the land now and only the blood of the unknown half-caste who had tried to steal their horse trickled in rivulets into the bed.

# IX

TANNER SAT AT HIS KITCHEN TABLE THE NEXT DAY LOOK-
ing out the window at the long driveway and the road. Watching
each vehicle to see if it was a bodytruck or one of the cars he knew.

Dusk settled upon the country and vehicles' headlights
blinked on and he watched the headlights draw along the road
then flash past his turn-off.

"They're not coming," said the slick-haired, leather-coat-
ed man who sat across from him. "You said by nightfall."

"It's only just nightfall."

"No one's coming."

Tanner swore under his breath. If Eccleston would ring
again ... Now the client was in the house, a phone call might count
for something.

But there was no call. And there was no truck.

"You said yourself these boys had messed you about in the
past. The black boy probably lied. I've never know one that told
the truth more than one time in three. They're born liars. It's in
their blood. You've been taken for a fool. And what's worse, I have
too. No one crosses me, August. Give me the money."

Tanner spat in to a handkerchief. He took his wallet out of
a drawer and took out a hundred-dollar note and thought his
trembling hand looked older than it ever had. He eyed the slick-
haired man over the table. He put the note down but kept it under
his hand.

The man began dialling on his mobile phone.

"We'll teach them a lesson. Make them keen to get us that horse."

"Who are you callin?"

"The boy I told you about. He works at the local supermarket. He's just got outta Borallon. I've got a friend who gives me the names of boys like him just as soon as they get out."

"What was he in for?"

The slick-haired man shrugged.

"Something sufficient to put him there. Don't worry. We'll teach the bastards a lesson, all right."

"They're not in town," said Tanner.

"The North boy is. He was at a dance here last night."

"How do you know that?"

"I've had this Borallon kid tracking them for a while now, just in case he was needed."

The man took his phone onto the veranda, spoke for a few minutes and then returned.

"The money."

Tanner pushed the note across the table.

"Can't I see this bastard?' said Tanner. "To speak to him?"

"It's best he doesn't see you and you don't see him."

The man took the money. "I'll put this in a mailbox up the road toward town. Can you think of a good one?"

"Frank Bertolotti's," Tanner said. "He's never home. It's a twenty-gallon drum. Easy to pick out. Half a mile north of here."

The slick-haired man nodded and smiled. Then the man's eyes became less friendly. "Don't mention this business to anyone, August. And whatever you do, don't mention my name."

Tanner nodded.

"Don't worry, August. The boy's under orders. He'll behave."

The man left and Tanner stood up to boil water for tea. His eyes travelled between the headlights on the road and the place where the hundred-dollar note had sat on the table in the darkening room.

GREY ROSE BEFORE Irene that morning and visited Vanessa at the cousin's house where she had stayed the night. Now she was driving back to prepare their move to the city. She wondered what her parents would say about her splitting with her fiancé after only a fortnight. "They'll hate it," she told Grey. "But they know me." She laughed and shook her head. She ended by making Grey promise he would come back with her. "At the end of the month," he said. And this time he meant it.

It was after three but he did not want to go home yet. He walked into town and sat long at the café over black tea, watching winter-dry and dirty Banjalang Street beneath an ashen sky, watching the lives of others while his own was suspended between Mary Smokes and what lay ahead. He stayed at the café until five o'clock. He thought of the boys and of all the evenings, no different in shape to this one, that they had spent and lost.

A few more people than usual were in town this evening for Christmas in July: tourists who already looked bored and wondered why they had come.

Grey decided not to attend the party that night. He had seen it many times before and his interest was all gone. He did not drive home or go to collect Irene from the restaurant. He had troubled her enough. He walked over the old railway tracks at the back of town to Mary Smokes Creek. He sat on the bank and watched rain spit into stagnant pools. A shaft of rose-coloured light came through a break in the cloud and lit a paddock where horses picked through winter clover. Then the light drained out of the day. A cold wind blew out of the western plains and drove a rack of clouds before it and he stood up and stared across the grass to the southeast and in that distance he saw two white buildings, formless and indecipherable, and he heard the faint dull roar of the highway, and all at once he was visited by the feeling that Eccleston and Irene were in trouble. Perhaps the kind that could not be handled alone. He reasoned the feeling could not be truth, yet it stayed with him. He spoke to Irene as though in prayer, as though she might truly be able to hear him. I can't

walk you tonight. Run home. Run straight home and don't stop.
As though ruin was waiting somewhere back there on the road,
where she herself might be waiting for him now, waiting for him
to come and walk her back to the house as he had done so many
times before. He ran back to his truck where it was parked at
Vanessa's cousin's. He drove south on the highway in the twilight.
His headlights lit the boy on the side of the road.

THE WIND MADE waves in the long yellow grass on the roadside.
The sun was almost gone and a mist of rain was settling in. She
had been waiting for her brother to come and collect her from the
Chinese restaurant. She had started walking home. At a distance
the two trucks looked alike, so she stopped and walked toward
the vehicle that followed her. She had been ready to tell him that
she knew he would not forget her.

She had been ready to tell him that
she knew he would not forget her.

The blond, stubble-bearded boy told her to get in. Now she
remembered where she had seen him: unpacking boxes at the
back of the supermarket on the highway when she went there with
Amy and Minh Quy.

She shook her head.

"I'm goin to your house. I've got to see your brother. Get in."

She turned and ran along the highway. The boy followed
her in the truck. She had made it almost to the gravel of her drive.
The car skidded off the side of the road into the grass and the
boy leapt out and grabbed her by the hair.

"Where's your brother, pretty?"

She shook her head. He did not ask again. He slapped her
face hard and threw her down in the grass. She scratched at
him. Blood from his cheek dripped onto her face. A look of animal
fury came into the boy's eyes. He could not bear her beauty and
the insult. He put a knife to her throat and told her to be quiet.
She screamed and when he covered her mouth and leant to kiss
her neck she bit his cheek.

"You filthy little slut!' he hissed. "You filthy bitch!"

And he drove the blade into her heart.

THE BOY STOOD up when the headlights were on him. Grey saw the blankness and shock in his face and the blood on his shirt, and tears burst from Grey's eyes. He took his shotgun from the mount at the back of the cabin and loaded and snapped the barrel closed and fired a shot that was meant for the heart but hit the boy's shoulder. The boy fell but raised himself and staggered back to his truck. Grey loaded another shell and fired and blew out the back window, but the truck sped off toward the highway and the night.

He threw away the gun. He cried out and held her to his chest.

He pushed a tear-wet lock of hair from her face that was wet with crying. He held her arms that were limp like a cloth doll's. Then he saw the blood on her dress, on her leg, running down to her feet into a small pool on the ground.

He screamed at her to speak to him but she could not. Already her eyes were clouded mirrors and he was not sure she saw him. She trembled violently. He felt her forehead that was cold. He picked her up and felt the discordance of spirit and body – that the creature who caused him the most pain in this world was made up of so little of it.

He put her little chin in his right hand and tried to make her look at him but she would not. Then her eyes closed. He cradled her in his arms and realized she did not know he was there. He saw again the places from which she bled, and he knew that this was all because she was too beautiful. He wiped away her tears and brushed her hair with his hand. Another trickle of blood ran down her leg. While he held her a cupful had leaked onto the yellow grass. She gasped and opened and closed her eyes a last time and he screamed that she could not die for a cupful of blood. And when she who he loved stopped breathing, so did he and he hoped he would die with her.

He screamed out Eccleston's name. He screamed into the wind but even from here he could see there was no truck in the

drive and no light on inside and the decrepit white house was
empty.

HE WALKED WITH her across the grass to the middle of the flat.
He sat down where the merry-go-round's coloured lights flickered through the eucalypts on the creek. He lay down with her and
looked up at the sky and from a few hundred yards and a world
away at Cormorant Bay he heard the faint strains of song. Children
who in his own time had performed the Nativity and now sang
popular songs. Excited cries meant a gaudy Santa Claus had come
to hand out gifts. Then came the fireworks. Roman candles shot
up over the lake where they burst and sprayed. The cinders fell
down and vanished on the water. Then the songs and the fireworks
were over. It was false Christmas. Only the merry-go-round was
left turning. In that northern distance the paint-chipped horses
turned without riders, the operator waiting on a few extra dollars
to close the day.

Grey had only this day felt strong, felt the human desire
to leave his handprint upon the world. Now he no longer wished
to convince the world of his presence or its error or of anything
else. In the day it had been far away and from far away he could
entertain it. Tonight it eyed him over its kill. Now she was in his
arms and further away than the stars. His only desire was to turn
back one hour and take what was his away somewhere in the
darkness. He would find Eccleston and they three who loved
would walk up into the hills, to a place where secrets could be
kept, and he would hold her in the storm that was coming and
never let her go.

Against the stars crept the pretty orange glow of the highway: those lights that admitted no secrets but tonight, the
secret identity of a killer. They droned away into the night like
permanence. Then it began to sprinkle rain and he could not
see the stars anywhere in heaven. The wind blew the rain around
a long time before it fell to earth. Winter rain in the town of
Mary Smokes or in any of the towns in that country was a rare

thing. Grey North sat up with his sister's body in his lap and looked at the water falling quietly out of the dark and thought that this would be a true storm. In time he shut his eyes and all he knew was the cold in the air and the absence of breath in her small body and the sound of the water beginning to rush in Mary Smokes Creek.

# X

BILL NORTH UNLOCKED THE ROOM HE RENTED ABOVE
the bar and picked up the letter that was slid under the door.
Angela Teal's name was on the back of the envelope. He flipped it
over and saw the postmark from a fortnight ago. He took it to
the window. He sat down in the chair where he had spent these
last three afternoons with a bottle, watching the sun descend
behind spindly black desert trees and a faded cemetery.

The letter said his pension had come through. Angela
wrote with genuine happiness. The money was more than they
had hoped. It seemed she would be able to take that holiday
overseas with her sister this year after all. She wrote that, though
she had not been home for a while, she planned to redecorate
the house before she left – to make it more like a home. She said
she meant to carpet the floors, and put a proper rack for coats
instead of "those bolts in the wall," and that if he did not mind she
would take down his former wife's Black Madonna "and that
terrible lamp that stains the walls. I know your daughter is nos-
talgic about those, but you'll agree children must grow up some-
time. I hope this is all right with you."

He put the letter on his lap and looked onto the darkening
plain. Yes, that is all right, he thought. He had been haunted too
long by ghosts.

"It doesn't matter," he said aloud, his blood-shot eyes taking
in the dying rays of the sun. "Maybe now there can be happiness." The happiness there could never be in the days of his wife,

when love had complicated everything and finally turned it all sour. He thought this as the first spits of a rare winter rain pock-marked the dust in the cemetery across the way. Then the western horizon was black. Fear stirred in him and he stood and let the letter blow out of his hands.

# Acknowledgements

SPECIAL THANKS TO POP, BUSH, LEE, TRIN, GRANDAD, Nan, Peter and John Sims, and Barry Scott. And with prayers for Stacey.